George Orwell

ANIMAL FARM

HERITAGE CLASSICS

George Orwell

ANIMAL FARM

HERITAGE PUBLISHERS
New Delhi

HERITAGE PUBLISHERS
19-A, Ansari Road, Daryaganj,
New Delhi - 110 002
Tel.: 23266258, 23264444
Fax.: 23263050
E-mail: info@heritagepublishers.in

ISBN: 81-7026-208-9

Printed in India

ORWELL'S PREFACE TO

ANIMAL FARM

The following essay was written as a preface to the first edition of Animal Farm but was not included in the published book and only discovered in the author's original typescript some years later. It is now a favourite citation for critics of our supposedly free press, as an illustration of how the media can work to suppress uncomfortable truths without this necessitating some vast conspiracy. It is "ironic" that the particular example of self-censorship Orwell refers to in the essay was the refusal of the left-wing and liberal press of the time to publish criticism of the Soviet Union - not a major feature of Western media orthodoxy in later years. Indeed, the subsequent popularity of Animal Farm and 1984 has much to do with their use in the latter sustained attack on the USSR or, more usually, "Communist Subversives" (or, more usually,

Such a usage is problematic; while Animal Farm is very clearly a deserved satire on the Soviet Union, 1984 is less an attack on the left than a satiric extrapolation drawn from the argument of James Burnham's The Managerial Revolution, which predicted the replacement of left/right ideology with a new ruling class of technocrats and social scientists. In any case, casting Orwell as a gadfly of Socialism requires serious distortion of his political viewpoint and the intention behind his works, but how dismaying Orwell would have found this is debatable. Given his (thoroughly justified) hatred of Stalinism. forged in the Spanish Civil War, where he witnessed the betrayal of the non-Stalinist Left by their pro-Russian "comrades", it is possible that Orwell would have made the same ideological journey Burnham did, from leftist to Cold Warrior, had he lived. Despite the consistency with which his work stated the principle of extending to our enemies the considerations and freedoms we consider indispensable for ourselves, Orwell spent part of his last years drawing up lists of those he considered Soviet pawns. Such McCarthyist behaviour from a long term champion of freedom and humanity suggests that the danger of sliding into "Fascist ways of thought", as he termed them, must be real indeed.

—Robert Weaver

THE FREEDOM OF THE PRESS

This book was first tought of, so far as the central idea goes, in 1937, but was not written down until about the end of 1943. By the time when it came to be written it was obvious that there would be great difficulty in getting it published (in spite of the present book shortage which ensures that anything describable as a book will 'sell'), and in the event it was refused by four publishers. Only one of these had any ideological motive. Two had been publishing anti-Russian books for years, and the other had no noticeable political colour. One publisher actually started by accepting the book, but after making the preliminary arrangements he decided to consult the Ministry of Information, who appear to have warned him, or at any rate strongly advised him, against publishing it. Here is an extract from his letter:

> I mentioned the reaction I had had from an important official in the Ministry of Information with regard to *Animal Farm*. I must confess that this expression of opinion has given me seriously to think..... I can see now that it might be regarded as something which it was highly ill-advised to publish at the present time. If the fable were addressed generally to dictators and dictatorships at large then publication would be all right, but the fable does follow, as I see now, so completely the progress of the Russian Soviets and their two dictators, that it

> can apply only to Russia, to the exclusion of the other dictatorships. Another thing: it would be less offensive if the predominant caste in the fable were not pigs. [It is not quite clear whether this suggested modification is Mr ... 's own idea, or originated with the Ministry of Information;but it seems to have the official ring about it -*Orwell's Note*] I think the choice of pigs as the ruling caste will no doubt give offence to many people, and particularly to anyone who is a bit touchy, as undoubtedly the Russians are.

This kind of thing is not a good symptom, Obviously it is not desirable that a government department should have any power of censorship (except security censorship, which no one objects to in war time) over books which are not officially sponsored. Bur rhe chief danger to freedom of thought and speech at this moment is not the direct interference of the MOI or any official body. If publishers and editors exert themselves to keep certain topics out of print, it is not because they are frightened of prosecution but because they are frightened of public opinion. In this country intellectual cowardice is the worst enemy a writer or journalist has to face, and that fact does not seem to me to have had the discussion it deserves.

Any fairminded person with journalistic experience will admit that during this war *official* censorship has not been particularly irksome. We have not been subjected to the kind of totalitarian 'co-ordination that it might have been reasonable to expect. The press has some justified grievances, but on the whole the Government has behaved well and has been surprisingly tolerant of minority opinions. The sinister fact about literary censorship in England is that it is largely voluntary. Unpopular ideas can be silenced, and inconvenient facts kept dark, without the need for any official ban. Anyone who has lived long in a foreign country will know of instances of sensational items of news - things which on their own merits would get the big headlines - being kept right out of the British press, not because the Government intervened but because of a general tacit agreement that 'it wouldn't do' to mention that particular fact. So far as the daily newspapers go, this is easy to understand. The British press is extremely centralized, and most of it is owned by wealthy men who have every motive to be dishonest on certain important topics. Bur the same kind of veiled censorship also operates in books and periodicals, as well as in plays, films and radio. At any given moment there is an orthodoxy, a body of ideas which it is assumed that all right-thinking people will accept without question, It is not exactly forbidden to say this, that or the other, but it is, not done' to say it, just as in mid-Victorian times it was 'not done' to mention trousers in the presence of a lady.Anyone who challenges the prevailing orthodoxy finds himself silenced with surprising effectiveness. A genuinely unfashionable opinion is almost never given a fair hearing, either in the popular press or in the highbrow periodicals.

At this moment what is demanded by the prevailing orthodoxy is an uncritical admiration of Soviet Russia. Everyone knows this, nearly everyone acts on it. Any serious criticism of the Soviet regime, any disclosure of facts which the Soviet government would prefer to keep hidden, is next door to unprintable. And this nation-wide conspiracy to flatter our ally takes place, curiously enough, against a background of genuine intellectual tolerance. For though you are not allowed to criticize the Soviet government, at least you are reasonably free to criticize our own. Hardly anyone will print an attack on Stalin, but it is quite safe to attack Churchill, at any rare in books and periodicals. And throughout five years of war, during two or three of which we were fighting for national survival, countless books, pamphlets and articles advocating a compromise peace have been published without interference. More, they have been published without exciting much disapproval. So long as the prestige of the USSR is not involved, the principle of free speech has been reasonably well upheld. There are other forbidden topics, and I shall mention some of them presently, but the prevailing attitude towards the USSR is much the most serious symptom. It is, as it were, spontaneous, and is not due to the action of any pressure group.

The servility with which the greater part of the English intelligentsia have swallowed and repeated Russian propaganda from 1941 onwards would be quite astounding if it were not that they have behaved similarly on several earlier occasions. On one controversial issue after another the Russian viewpoint has been accepted without examination and then publicized with complete disregard to historical truth or intellectual decency. To name only one instance, the BBC celebrated the twenty-fifth anniversary of the Red Army without mentioning Trotsky. This was about as accurate as commemorating the battle of Trafalgar without mentioning Nelson, but it evoked no protest from the English intelligentsia. In the internal struggles in the various occupied countries, the British press has in almost all cases sided with the faction favoured by the Russians and libelled the opposing faction, sometimes suppressing material evidence in order to do so. A particularly glaring case was that of Colonel Mihailovich, the Jugoslav Chetnik leader. The Russians, who had their own Jugoslav protege in Marshal Tito, accused Mihailovich of collaborating with the Germans. This accusation was promptly taken up by the British press: Mihailovichs supporters were given no chance of answering it, and facts contradicting it were simply kept out of print. In July of 1943 the Germans offered a reward of 100,000 gold crowns for the capture of Tito, and a similar reward for the capture of Mihailovich. The British press 'splashed' the reward for Tito, but only one paper mentioned (in small print) the reward for Mihailovich: and the charges of collaborating with the Germans continued. Very similar things happened during the Spanish civil war.Then, too, the factions on the Republican side which the Russians were determined to crush were recklessly libelled in the English leftwing press, and any statement in their defence even in letter form, was refused publication.At present, not only is serious criticism of the USSR considered reprehensible,but even the fact of che existence of such criticism is kept secret in some cases.

For example, shortly before his death Trotsky had written a biography of Stalin. One may assume that it was not an altogether unbiased book, but obviously it was saleable. An American publisher had arranged to issue it and the book was in print - I believe rhe review copies had been sent out - when the USSR entered the war. The book was immediately withdrawn. Not a word about this has ever appeared in the British press, though clearly the existence of such a book, and its suppression, was a news item worth a few paragraphs.

It is important to distinguish between the kind of censorship that the English literary intelligentsia voluntarily impose upon themselves, and the censorship that can sometimes be enforced by pressure groups. Notoriously, certain topics cannot be discussed because of 'vested interests'. The best-known case is the patent medicine racket. Again, the Catholic Church has considerable influence in the press and can silence criticism of itself to some extent. A scandal involving a Catholic priest is almost never given publicity, whereas an Anglican priest who gets into trouble (e.g. the Rector of Stiffkey) is headline news. It is very rare for anything of an anti-Catholic tendency to appear on the stage or in a film. Any actor can tell you that a play or film which attacks or makes fun of the Catholic Church is liable to be boycotted in the press and will probably be a failure. But this kind of thing is harmless, or at least it is understandable. Any large organization will look after its own interests as best it can. and overr propaganda is not a thing to object to. One would no more expect the *Daily Worker* to publicize unfavourable facts about the USSR than one would expect the *Catholic-Herald*-to denounce the Pope. But then every thinking person knows the *Daily Worker* and the *Catholic Herald for* what they are. What is disquieting is that where the USSR and its policies are concerned one cannot expect intelligent criticism or even, in many cases, plain honesty from Liberal writers and journalists who are under no direct pressure to falsify their opinions. Stalin is sacrosanct and certain aspects of his policy must not be seriously discussed. This rule has been almost universally observed since 1941, but it had operated, to a greater extent than is sometimes realized, for ten years earlier than that. Throughout that time, criticism of the Soviet regime from *the left* could only obtain a hearing with difficulty. There was a huge output of anti-Russian literature, but nearly all of it was from the Conservative angle and manifestly dishonest, out of date and actuated by sordid motives. On the other side there was an equally huge and almost equally dishonest stream of pro-Russian propaganda, and what amounted to a boycott on anyone who tried to discuss all-important questions in a grown-up manner. You could, indeed, publish anti-Russian books, but to do so was to make sure of being ignored or misrepresented by nearly the whole of the highbrow press. Both publicly and privately you were warned that it was 'not done'. What you said might possibly be true, but it was 'inopportune' and 'played into the hands of this or that reactionary interest. This attitude was usually defended on the ground that the international situation, and the urgent need for an Anglo-Russian alliance, demanded it; but it was clear that this was a rationalization. The English intelligentsia, or a great part of it, had developed a nationalistic loyalty towards the USSR, and in their hearts they felt that to cast any doubt on the wisdom of Stalin was a kind of blasphemy. Events in Russia and events elsewhere were to be judged by different standards. The endless executions in the purses of 1936-8 were applauded by life-long opponents of capital punishment, and it was considered equally proper ro publicize famines when they happened in India and to conceal them when they happened in the Ukraine. And if this was true before the war, the intellectual atmosphere is certainly no better now.

But now to come back to this book of mine. the reaction towards it of most English intellectuals will be quite simple: It oughtn't to have been published'. Naturally, those reviewers who understand the art of denigration will not attack it on political grounds but on literary ones. They will say that it is a dull, siliy book and a disgraceful waste of paper. This may well be true, but it is obviously not the whole of the story. One does not say that a book 'ought not to have been published' merely because it is a bad book. After all, acres of rubbish are printed daily and no one bothers. The English intelligentsia, or most of them, will object to this book because it traduces their Leader and (as they see it) does harm to the cause of progress. If it did the opposite they would have nothing to say against it, even if its literary faults were ten times as glaring as they are The success of, for instance, the Left Book Club over a period of four or five years shows how willing they are to tolerate both scurrility and slipshod writing. provided that it tells them what they want to hear.

The issue involved here is quite a simple one: Is every opinion, however unpopular - however foolish, even - entitled to a hearing? Put it in that form and nearly any English intellectual will feel that he ought to say 'Yes'. But give it a concrete shape, and ask, 'How about an attack on Stalin? Is *that* entitled to a hearing?', and the answer more often than not will be 'No'. In that case the current orthodoxy happens to be challenged, and *so* the principle of free speech lapses. Now, when one demands liberty of speech and of the press, one is not demanding absolute liberty-. There always must be, or at any rate there always will be, some degree of censorship, so long as organized societies endure. But freedom, as Rosa Luxembourg said, is 'freedom for the other fellow'.The same principle is contained in the famous words of Voltaire: 'I detest what you say; I will defend to the death your right to say it'. If the intellectual liberty which without a doubt has been one of the distinguishing marks of western civilization means anything at ail, it means that everyone shall have the right to say and to print what he believes to be the truth, provided only that it does not harm the rest of the community in some quite unmistakable way. Both capitalist democracy and the western versions of Socialism have till recently taken that principle for granted.Our Government, as I have already pointed out, still makes some show of respecting it. The ordinary people in the street - partly, perhaps, because they are not sufficiently interested in ideas to be intolerant about them - still vaguely hold that 'I suppose everyone's got a right to their own opinion, It is only, or at any rate it is chiefly, the literary and scientific intelligentsia, the very people who ought to be the guardians of liberty, who are beginning to despise it, in theory as well as in practice.

One of the peculiar phenomena of our time is the renegade Liberal. Over and above the familiar Marxist claim that 'bourgeois liberty' is an illusion, there is now a widespread tendency to argue that one can only defend democracy by totalitarian methods. If one loves democracy, the argument runs, one must crush its enemies by no matter what means. And who are its enemies? It always appears that they are not only those who attack it openly and consciously, but those who 'objectively' endanger it by spreading mistaken doctrines, in other words, defending democracy involves destroying all independence of thought. This argument was used, for instance, to justify the Russian purges. The most ardent Russophile hardly believed that all of the victims were guilty of all the things they were accused of. but by holding heretical opinions they 'objectively harmed the regime, and therefore it was quite right not only to massacre them but to discredit them by false accusations. The same argument was used to justify the quite conscious lying that went on in the leftwing press about the Trotskyists and other Republican minorities in the Spanish civil war, And it was used again as a reason for yelping against *habeas corpus* when Mosley was released in 1943.

These people don't see that if you encourage totalitarian methods, the time may come when they will be used against you instead of for you. Make a habit of imprisoning Fascists without trial, and perhaps the process won't srop at Fascists. Soon after the suppressed *Daily Worker* had been reinstated, 1 was lecturing to a working-men's college in South London.

The audience were working-class and lower-middle class intellectuals - the same sort of audience that one used to meet at Left Book Club branches. The lecture had touched on the Freedom of the press, and at the end, to my astonishment, several questioners stood up and asked me: Did I not think that the lifting of the ban on the *Daily Worker* was a great mistake? When asked why, they said that it was a paper of doubtful loyalty and ought not to be tolerated in war time. I found myself defending the *Daily Worker,* which has gone out of its way to libel me more than once. But where had these people learned this essentially totalitarian outlook? Pretty certainly they had learned it from the Communists themselves! Tolerance and decency are deeply rooted in England, but they are not indestructible, and they have to be kept alive partly by conscious effort. The result of preaching totalitarian doctrines is to weaken the instinct by means of which free peoples know what is or is not dangerous. The case of Mosley illustrates this. In 1940 it was perfectly right to intern Mosley, whether or not he had committed any technical crime. We were fighring for our lives and could not allow a possible quisling to go free. To keep him shut up, without trial, in 1943 was an outrage. The general failure to see this was a bad symptom, though it is true that the agitation against Mosley's release was partly factitious and partly a rationalization of other discontents. But how much of the present slide towards Fascist ways of thought is traceable to the 'anti-Fascism' of the past ten years and the unscrupulousness it has entailed?

It is important to realize that the current Russomania is

only a symptom of the general weakening of the western liberal tradition. Had the MOI chipped in and definitely vetoed the publication of this book, the bulk of The English intelligentsia would have seen nothing disquieting in this. Uncritical loyalty to the USSR happens to be the current orthodoxy, and where the supposed Interests of the USSR are Involved they are willing to tolerate not only censorship but the deliberate falsification of history. To name one instance. At the death of John Reed, the author of *Ten Days that Shook the World* ' first-hand account of the early days of the Russian Revolution - the copyright of the book passed into the hands of the British Communist Party, to whom 1 believe Reed had bequeathed it. Some years later the British Communists, having destroyed the original edition of rhe book as completely as they could, issued garbled version from which they had eliminated mentions of Trotsky and also omitted the Introduction written by Lenin. If a radical intelligentsia had still existed in Britain, this act of forgery would have been exposed and denounced in every literary paper in the country. As it was there was little or no protest. To many English intellectuals it seemed quite a natural thing to, do. And this tolerance or *[of?}* plain dishonesty means much more than that admiration for Russia happens to be fashionable at this moment. Quite possibly that particular fashion will not last. For all I know. by the time this book is published my view of the Soviet regime may be the generally-accepted one. But what use would that be in itself? To exchange one orthodoxy for another is not necessarily an advance. The enemy is the gramophone mind, whether or not one agrees with the record that is being played at the moment.

I am well acquainted with all the arguments .against freedom of thought and speech – the arguments which claim chat it cannot exist, and the arguments which claim that it ought nor to. I answer simply that they don't convince me and that our civilization over a period of four hundred years has been founded on the opposite notice. For quite a decade past I have believed that the existing Russian regime is a mainly evil thing, and I claim the right to say so, in spite of the fact char we are allies with the USSR in a war which I want to see won. if I had to choose a test to justify myself, 1 should choose the line from Milton:

By the known rules of ancient liberty.

The word ancient emphasizes the fact that intellectual freedom is a deep-roored tradition without which our characteristic western culture could only doubtfully exist. From that tradition many of onr intellectuals are visibly turning away. They have accepted the principle that a book should be published or suppressed, praised or damned, not on its merits bur according to political expediency. And others who do not actually hold this view assent to it from sheer cowardice. An example of this is the failure of the numerous and vocal English pacifists to raise their voices against the prevalent worship of Russian militarism.According to those pacifists, all violence is evil and they have urged us at every' stage of the war to give in or at least to make a compromise peace. But how many of them have ever suggested that war is also evil when it is waged *by* the Red Army? Apparently the Russians have a right to defend themselves,whereas for us to do *[so}* is a deadly sin. One can only explain this contradiction in one way: that is, by a cowardly desire to keep in with the bulk of the Intelligentsia, whose patriotism is directed towards the USSR rather than towards Britain. I know that the English intelligentsia have plenty of reason for their timidity and dishonesty, indeed I know by heart the arguments by which they justify' themselves. But at least let us have no more nonsense about defending liberty against Fascism. If liberty means anything at all it means the right to tell people what they do not want to hear. The common people still vaguely subscribe to that doctrine and act on it. In our country - it is not the same in all countries: it was not so in republican France, and it is not so in the USA today *[i.e. 1945*(!) - it is the liberals who fear liberty and the intellectuals who want to do dirt oil the intellect: it is to draw attention to that fact that I have written this preface.

Chapter I

Mr. Jones, of the Manor Farm, had locked the hen-houses for the night, but was too drunk to remember to shut the popholes. With the ring of light from his lantern dancing from side to side, he lurched across the yard, kicked off his boots at the back door, drew himself a last glass of beer from the barrel in the scullery, and made his way up to bed, where Mrs. Jones was already snoring.

As soon as the light in the bedroom went out there was a stirring and a fluttering all through the farm buildings. Word had gone round during the day that old Major, the prize Middle White boar, had had a strange dream on the previous night and wished to communicate it to the other animals. It had been agreed that they should all meet in the big barn as soon as Mr. Jones was safely out of the way. Old Major (so he was always called, though the name under which he had been exhibited was Willingdon Beauty) was so highly regarded on the farm that everyone was quite ready to lose an hour's sleep in order to hear what he had to say.

At one end of the big barn, on a sort of raised platform, Major was already ensconced on his bed of straw, under a lantern which hung from a beam. He was twelve years old and had lately grown rather stout, but he was still a majestic-looking pig, with a wise and benevolent appearance in spite of the fact that his tushes had never been cut. Before long the other animals began to arrive and make themselves comfortable after their different fashions. First came the three dogs, Bluebell, Jessie, and Pincher, and then the pigs, who settled down in the straw immediately in front of the platform. The hens perched themselves on the window-sills, the pigeons fluttered up to the rafters, the sheep and cows lay down behind the pigs and began to chew the cud. The two cart-horses, Boxer and Clover, came in together, walking very slowly and setting down their vast hairy hoofs with great care lest there should be some small animal concealed in the straw. Clover was a stout motherly mare approaching middle life, who had never quite got her figure back after her fourth foal. Boxer was an enormous beast, nearly eighteen hands high, and as strong as any two ordinary horses put together. A white stripe down his nose gave him a somewhat stupid appearance, and in fact he was not of first-rate intelligence, but he was universally respected for his steadiness of character and tremendous powers of work. After the horses came Muriel, the white goat, and Benjamin, the donkey. Benjamin was the oldest animal on the farm, and the worst tempered. He seldom talked, and when he did, it was usually to make some cynical remark—for instance, he would say that God had given him a tail to keep the flies off, but that he would sooner have had no tail and no flies. Alone among the animals on the farm he never laughed. If asked why, he would say that he saw nothing to laugh at. Nevertheless, without openly admitting it, he was devoted to Boxer; the two of them usually spent their Sundays together in the small paddock beyond the orchard, grazing side by side and never speaking.

The two horses had just lain down when a brood of ducklings, which had lost their mother, filed into the barn, cheeping feebly and wandering from side to side to find some place where they would not be trodden on. Clover made a sort of wall round them with her great foreleg, and the ducklings nestled down inside it and promptly fell asleep. At the last moment Mollie, the foolish, pretty white mare who drew Mr. Jones's trap, came mincing daintily in, chewing at a lump of sugar. She took a place near the front and began flirting her white mane, hoping to draw attention to the red ribbons it was plaited with. Last of all came the cat, who looked round, as usual, for the warmest place, and finally squeezed herself in between Boxer and Clover; there she purred contentedly throughout Major's speech without listening to a word of what he was saying.

All the animals were now present except Moses, the tame raven, who slept on a perch behind the back door. When Major saw that they had all made themselves comfortable and were waiting attentively, he cleared his throat and began:

"Comrades, you have heard already about the strange dream that I had last night. But I will come to the dream later. I have something else to say first. I do not think, comrades, that I shall be with you for many months longer, and before I die, I feel it my duty to pass on to you such wisdom as I have acquired. I have had a long life, I have had much time for thought as I lay alone in my stall, and I think I may say that I understand the nature of life on this earth as well as any animal now living. It is about this that I wish to speak to you.

"Now, comrades, what is the nature of this life of ours? Let us face it: our lives are miserable, laborious, and short. We are born, we are given just so much food as will keep the breath in our bodies, and those of us who are capable of it are forced to work to the last atom of our strength; and the very instant that our usefulness has come to an end we are slaughtered with hideous cruelty. No animal in England knows the meaning of happiness or leisure after he is a year old. No animal in England is free. The life of an animal is misery and slavery: that is the plain truth.

"But is this simply part of the order of nature? Is it because this land of ours is so poor that it cannot afford a decent life to those who dwell upon it? No, comrades, a thousand times no! The soil of England is fertile, its climate is good, it is capable of affording food in abundance to an enormously greater number of animals than now inhabit it. This single farm of ours would support a dozen horses, twenty cows, hundreds of sheep—and all of them living in a comfort and a dignity that are now almost beyond our imagining. Why then do we continue in this miserable condition? Because nearly the whole of the produce of our labour is stolen from us by human beings. There, comrades, is the answer to all our problems. It is summed up in a single word—Man. Man is the only real enemy we have. Remove Man from the scene, and the root cause of hunger and overwork is abolished for ever.

"Man is the only creature that consumes without producing. He does not give milk, he does not lay eggs, he is too weak to pull the plough, he cannot run fast enough to catch rabbits. Yet he is lord of all the animals. He sets them to work, he gives back to them the bare minimum that will prevent them from starving, and the rest he keeps for himself. Our labour tills the soil, our dung fertilises it, and yet there is not one of us that owns more than his bare skin. You cows that I see before me, how many thousands of gallons of milk have you given during this last year? And what has happened to that milk which should have been breeding up sturdy calves? Every drop of it has gone down the throats of our enemies. And you hens, how many eggs have you laid in this last year, and how many of those eggs ever hatched into chickens? The rest have all gone to market to bring in money for Jones and his men. And you, Clover, where are those four foals you bore, who should have been the support and pleasure of your old age? Each was sold at a year old—you will never see one of them again. In return for your four confinements and all your labour in the fields, what have you ever had except your bare rations and a stall?

"And even the miserable lives we lead are not allowed to reach their natural span. For myself I do not grumble, for I am one of the lucky ones. I am twelve years old and have had over four hundred children. Such is the natural life of a pig. But no animal escapes the cruel knife in the end. You young porkers who are sitting in front of me, every one of you will scream your lives out at the block within a year. To that horror we all must come—cows, pigs, hens, sheep, everyone. Even the horses and the dogs have no better fate. You, Boxer, the very day that those great muscles of yours lose their power, Jones will sell you to the knacker, who will cut your throat and boil you down for the foxhounds. As for the dogs, when they grow old and toothless, Jones ties a brick round their necks and drowns them in the nearest pond.

"Is it not crystal clear, then, comrades, that all the evils of this life of ours spring from the tyranny of human beings? Only get rid of Man, and the produce of our labour would be our own. Almost overnight we could become rich and free. What then must we do? Why, work night and day, body and soul, for the overthrow of the human race! That is my message to you, comrades: Rebellion! I do not know when that Rebellion will come, it might be in a week or in a hundred years, but I know, as surely as I see this straw beneath my feet, that sooner or later justice will be done. Fix your eyes on that, comrades, throughout the short remainder of your lives! And above all, pass on this message of mine to those who come after you, so that future generations shall carry on the struggle until it is victorious.

"And remember, comrades, your resolution must never falter. No argument must lead you astray. Never listen when they tell you that Man and the animals have a common interest, that the prosperity of the one is the prosperity of the others. It is all lies. Man serves the interests of no creature except himself. And among us animals let there be perfect unity, perfect comradeship in the struggle. All men are enemies. All animals are comrades."

At this moment there was a tremendous uproar. While Major was speaking four large rats had crept out of their holes and were sitting on their hindquarters, listening to him. The dogs had suddenly caught sight of them, and it was only by a swift dash for their holes that the rats saved their lives. Major raised his trotter for silence.

"Comrades," he said, "here is a point that must be settled. The wild creatures, such as rats and rabbits—are they our friends or our enemies? Let us put it to the vote. I propose this question to the meeting: Are rats comrades?"

The vote was taken at once, and it was agreed by an overwhelming majority that rats were comrades. There were only four dissentients, the three dogs and the cat, who was afterwards discovered to have voted on both sides. Major continued:

"I have little more to say. I merely repeat, remember always your duty of enmity towards Man and all his ways. Whatever goes upon two legs is an enemy. Whatever goes upon four legs, or has wings, is a friend. And remember also that in fighting against Man, we must not come to resemble him. Even when you have conquered him, do not adopt his vices. No animal must ever live in a house, or sleep in a bed, or wear clothes, or drink alcohol, or smoke tobacco, or touch money, or engage in trade. All the habits of Man are evil. And, above all, no animal must ever tyrannise over his own kind. Weak or strong, clever or simple, we are all brothers. No animal must ever kill any other animal. All animals are equal.

"And now, comrades, I will tell you about my dream of last night. I cannot describe that dream to you. It was a dream of the earth as it will be when Man has vanished. But it reminded me of something that I had long forgotten. Many years ago, when I was a little pig, my mother and the other sows used to sing an old song of which they knew only the tune and the first three words. I had known that tune in my infancy, but it had long since passed out of my mind. Last night, however, it came back to me in my dream. And what is more, the words of the song also came back—words, I am certain, which were sung by the animals of long ago and have been lost to memory for generations. I will sing you that song now, comrades. I am old and my voice is hoarse, but when I have taught you the tune, you can sing it better for yourself. It is called *Beasts of England.*"

Old Major cleared his throat and began to sing. As he had said, his voice was hoarse, but he sang well enough, and it was a stirring tune, something between *Clementine and La Cucaracha*. The words ran:

Beasts of England, beasts of Ireland,
Beasts of every land and clime,
Hearken to my joyful tidings
Of the golden future time.

Soon or late the day is coming,
Tyrant Man shall be o'erthrown,
And the fruitful fields of England
Shall be trod by beasts alone.

Rings shall vanish from our noses,
And the harness from our back,
Bit and spur shall rust forever,
Cruel whips no more shall crack.

Riches more than mind can picture,
Wheat and barley, oats and hay,
Clover, beans, and mangel-wurzels
Shall be ours upon that day.

Bright will shine the fields of En-
gland,
Purer shall its waters be,
Sweeter yet shall blow its breezes
On the day that sets us free.

For that day we all must labour,
Though we die before it break;
Cows and horses, geese and turkeys,
All must toil for freedom's sake.

Beasts of England, beasts of Ireland,
Beasts of every land and clime,
Hearken well and spread my tidings
Of the golden future time.

The singing of this song threw the animals into the wildest excitement. Almost before Major had reached the end, they had begun singing it for themselves. Even the stupidest of them had already picked up the tune and a few of the words, and as for the clever ones, such as the pigs and dogs, they had the entire song by heart within a few minutes. And then, after a few preliminary tries, the whole farm burst out into *Beasts of England* in tremendous unison. The cows lowed it, the dogs whined it, the sheep bleated it, the horses whinnied it, the ducks quacked it. They were so delighted with the song that they sang it right through five times in succession, and might have continued singing it all night if they had not been interrupted.

Unfortunately, the uproar awoke Mr. Jones, who sprang out of bed, making sure that there was a fox in the yard. He seized the gun which always stood in a corner of his bed-room, and let fly a charge of number 6 shot into the dark-ness. The pellets buried themselves in the wall of the barn and the meeting broke up hurriedly. Everyone fled to his own sleeping-place. The birds jumped on to their perches, the animals settled down in the straw, and the whole farm was asleep in a moment.

Chapter II

Three nights later old Major died peacefully in his sleep. His body was buried at the foot of the orchard.

This was early in March. During the next three months there was much secret activity. Major's speech had given to the more intelligent animals on the farm a completely new outlook on life. They did not know when the Rebellion predicted by Major would take place, they had no reason for thinking that it would be within their own lifetime, but they saw clearly that it was their duty to prepare for it. The work of teaching and organising the others fell naturally upon the pigs, who were generally recognised as being the cleverest of the animals. Pre-eminent among the pigs were two young boars named Snowball and Napoleon, whom Mr. Jones was breeding up for sale. Napoleon was a large, rather fierce-looking Berkshire boar, the only Berkshire on the farm, not much of a talker, but with a reputation for getting his own way. Snowball was a more vivacious pig than Napoleon, quicker in speech and more inventive, but was not considered to have the same depth of character. All the other male pigs on the farm were porkers. The best known among them was a small fat pig named Squealer, with very round cheeks, twinkling eyes, nimble movements, and a shrill voice. He was a brilliant talker, and when he was arguing some difficult point he had a way of skipping from side to side and whisking his tail which was somehow very persuasive. The others said of Squealer that he could turn black into white.

These three had elaborated old Major's teachings into a complete system of thought, to which they gave the name of Animalism. Several nights a week, after Mr. Jones was asleep, they held secret meetings in the barn and expounded the principles of Animalism to the others. At the beginning they met with much stupidity and apathy. Some of the animals talked of the duty of loyalty to Mr. Jones, whom they referred to as "Master," or made elementary remarks such as "Mr. Jones feeds us. If he were gone, we should starve to death." Others asked such questions as "Why should we care what happens after we are dead?" or "If this Rebellion is to happen anyway, what difference does it make whether we work for it or not?", and the pigs had great difficulty in making them see that this was contrary to the spirit of Animalism. The stupidest questions of all were asked by Mollie, the white mare. The very first question she asked Snowball was: "Will there still be sugar after the Rebellion?"

"No," said Snowball firmly. "We have no means of making sugar on this farm. Besides, you do not need sugar. You will have all the oats and hay you want."

"And shall I still be allowed to wear ribbons in my mane?" asked Mollie.

"Comrade," said Snowball, "those ribbons that you are so devoted to are the badge of slavery. Can you not understand that liberty is worth more than ribbons? "

Mollie agreed, but she did not sound very convinced.

The pigs had an even harder struggle to counteract the lies put about by Moses, the tame raven. Moses, who was

Mr. Jones's especial pet, was a spy and a tale-bearer, but he was also a clever talker. He claimed to know of the existence of a mysterious country called Sugarcandy Mountain, to which all animals went when they died. It was situated somewhere up in the sky, a little distance beyond the clouds, Moses said. In Sugarcandy Mountain it was Sunday seven days a week, clover was in season all the year round, and lump sugar and linseed cake grew on the hedges. The animals hated Moses because he told tales and did no work, but some of them believed in Sugarcandy Mountain, and the pigs had to argue very hard to persuade them that there was no such place.

Their most faithful disciples were the two cart-horses, Boxer and Clover. These two had great difficulty in thinking anything out for themselves, but having once accepted the pigs as their teachers, they absorbed everything that they were told, and passed it on to the other animals by simple arguments. They were unfailing in their attendance at the secret meetings in the barn, and led the singing of *Beasts of England,* with which the meetings always ended.

Now, as it turned out, the Rebellion was achieved much earlier and more easily than anyone had expected. In past years Mr. Jones, although a hard master, had been a capable farmer, but of late he had fallen on evil days. He had become much disheartened after losing money in a lawsuit, and had taken to drinking more than was good for him. For whole days at a time he would lounge in his Windsor chair in the kitchen, reading the newspapers, drinking, and occasionally feeding Moses on crusts of bread soaked in beer. His men were idle and dishonest, the fields were full of weeds, the buildings wanted roofing, the hedges were neglected, and the animals were underfed.

June came and the hay was almost ready for cutting. On Midsummer's Eve, which was a Saturday, Mr. Jones went into Willingdon and got so drunk at the Red Lion that he did not come back till midday on Sunday. The men had milked the cows in the early morning and then had gone out rabbiting, without bothering to feed the animals. When Mr. Jones got back he immediately went to sleep on the drawing-room sofa with the *News of the World* over his face, so that when evening came, the animals were still unfed. At last they could stand it no longer. One of the cows broke in the door of the store-shed with her horn and all the animals began to help themselves from the bins. It was just then that Mr. Jones woke up. The next moment he and his four men were in the store-shed with whips in their hands, lashing out in all directions. This was more than the hungry animals could bear. With one accord, though nothing of the kind had been planned beforehand, they flung themselves upon their tormentors. Jones and his men suddenly found themselves being butted and kicked from all sides. The situation was quite out of their control. They had never seen animals behave like this before, and this sudden uprising of creatures whom they were used to thrashing and maltreating just as they chose, frightened them almost out of their wits. After only a moment or two they gave up trying to defend themselves and took to their heels. A minute later all five of them were in full flight down the cart-track that led to the main road, with the animals pursuing them in triumph.

Mrs. Jones looked out of the bedroom window, saw what

was happening, hurriedly flung a few possessions into a carpet bag, and slipped out of the farm by another way. Moses sprang off his perch and flapped after her, croaking loudly. Meanwhile the animals had chased Jones and his men out on to the road and slammed the five-barred gate behind them. And so, almost before they knew what was happening, the Rebellion had been successfully carried through: Jones was expelled, and the Manor Farm was theirs.

For the first few minutes the animals could hardly believe in their good fortune. Their first act was to gallop in a body right round the boundaries of the farm, as though to make quite sure that no human being was hiding anywhere upon it; then they raced back to the farm buildings to wipe out the last traces of Jones's hated reign. The harness-room at the end of the stables was broken open; the bits, the nose-rings, the dog-chains, the cruel knives with which Mr. Jones had been used to castrate the pigs and lambs, were all flung down the well. The reins, the halters, the blinkers, the degrading nosebags, were thrown on to the rubbish fire which was burning in the yard. So were the whips. All the animals capered with joy when they saw the whips going up in flames. Snowball also threw on to the fire the ribbons with which the horses' manes and tails had usually been decorated on market days.

"Ribbons," he said, "should be considered as clothes, which are the mark of a human being. All animals should go naked."

When Boxer heard this he fetched the small straw hat which he wore in summer to keep the flies out of his ears, and flung it on to the fire with the rest.

In a very little while the animals had destroyed everything that reminded them of Mr. Jones. Napoleon then led them back to the store-shed and served out a double ration of corn to everybody, with two biscuits for each dog. Then they sang *Beasts of England* from end to end seven times running, and after that they settled down for the night and slept as they had never slept before.

But they woke at dawn as usual, and suddenly remembering the glorious thing that had happened, they all raced out into the pasture together. A little way down the pasture there was a knoll that commanded a view of most of the farm. The animals rushed to the top of it and gazed round them in the clear morning light. Yes, it was theirs—everything that they could see was theirs! In the ecstasy of that thought they gambolled round and round, they hurled themselves into the air in great leaps of excitement. They rolled in the dew, they cropped mouthfuls of the sweet summer grass, they kicked up clods of the black earth and snuffed its rich scent. Then they made a tour of inspection of the whole farm and surveyed with speechless admiration the ploughland, the hayfield, the orchard, the pool, the spinney. It was as though they had never seen these things before, and even now they could hardly believe that it was all their own.

Then they filed back to the farm buildings and halted in silence outside the door of the farmhouse. That was theirs too, but they were frightened to go inside. After a moment, however, Snowball and Napoleon butted the door open with their shoulders and the animals entered in single file, walking with the utmost care for fear of disturbing anything. They tiptoed from room to room, afraid to speak above a whisper and gazing with a kind of awe at the unbelievable luxury, at the beds with their feather mattresses, the looking-glasses, the horsehair sofa, the Brussels carpet, the lithograph of Queen Victoria over the drawing-room mantelpiece. They were just coming down the stairs when Mollie was discovered to be missing. Going back, the others found that she had remained behind in the best bedroom. She had taken a piece of blue ribbon from Mrs. Jones's dressing-table, and was holding it against her shoulder and admiring herself in the glass in a very foolish manner. The others reproached her sharply, and they went outside. Some hams hanging in the kitchen were taken out for burial, and the barrel of beer in the scullery was stove in with a kick from Boxer's hoof,—otherwise nothing in the house was touched. A unanimous resolution was passed on the spot that the farmhouse should be preserved as a museum. All were agreed that no animal must ever live there.

The animals had their breakfast, and then Snowball and Napoleon called them together again.

"Comrades," said Snowball, "it is half-past six and we have a long day before us. Today we begin the hay harvest. But there is another matter that must be attended to first."

The pigs now revealed that during the past three months they had taught themselves to read and write from an old spelling book which had belonged to Mr. Jones's children and which had been thrown on the rubbish heap. Napoleon sent for pots of black and white paint and led the way down to the five-barred gate that gave on to the main road. Then Snowball (for it was Snowball who was best at writing) took a brush between the two knuckles of his trotter, painted out

MANOR FARM from the top bar of the gate and in its place painted ANIMAL FARM. This was to be the name of the farm from now onwards. After this they went back to the farm buildings, where Snowball and Napoleon sent for a ladder which they caused to be set against the end wall of the big barn. They explained that by their studies of the past three months the pigs had succeeded in reducing the principles of Animalism to Seven Commandments. These Seven Commandments would now be inscribed on the wall; they would form an unalterable law by which all the animals on Animal Farm must live for ever after. With some difficulty (for it is not easy for a pig to balance himself on a ladder) Snowball climbed up and set to work, with Squealer a few rungs below him holding the paint-pot. The Commandments were written on the tarred wall in great white letters that could be read thirty yards away. They ran thus:

THE SEVEN COMMANDMENTS

1. *Whatever goes upon two legs is an enemy.*
2. *Whatever goes upon four legs, or has wings, is a friend.*
3. *No animal shall wear clothes.*
4. *No animal shall sleep in a bed.*
5. *No animal shall drink alcohol.*
6. *No animal shall kill any other animal.*
7. *All animals are equal.*

It was very neatly written, and except that "friend" was written "freind" and one of the "S's" was the wrong way round, the spelling was correct all the way through. Snowball read it aloud for the benefit of the others. All the animals nodded in complete agreement, and the cleverer ones at once began to learn the Commandments by heart.

"Now, comrades," cried Snowball, throwing down the paint-brush, "to the hayfield! Let us make it a point of honour to get in the harvest more quickly than Jones and his men could do."

But at this moment the three cows, who had seemed uneasy for some time past, set up a loud lowing. They had not been milked for twenty-four hours, and their udders were almost bursting. After a little thought, the pigs sent for buckets and milked the cows fairly successfully, their trotters being well adapted to this task. Soon there were five buckets of frothing creamy milk at which many of the animals looked with considerable interest.

"What is going to happen to all that milk?" said someone.

"Jones used sometimes to mix some of it in our mash," said one of the hens.

"Never mind the milk, comrades!" cried Napoleon, placing himself in front of the buckets. "That will be attended to. The harvest is more important. Comrade Snowball will lead the way. I shall follow in a few minutes. Forward, comrades! The hay is waiting."

So the animals trooped down to the hayfield to begin the harvest, and when they came back in the evening it was noticed that the milk had disappeared.

Chapter III

How they toiled and sweated to get the hay in! But their efforts were rewarded, for the harvest was an even bigger success than they had hoped.

Sometimes the work was hard; the implements had been designed for human beings and not for animals, and it was a great drawback that no animal was able to use any tool that involved standing on his hind legs. But the pigs were so clever that they could think of a way round every difficulty. As for the horses, they knew every inch of the field, and in fact understood the business of mowing and raking far better than Jones and his men had ever done. The pigs did not actually work, but directed and supervised the others. With their superior knowledge it was natural that they should assume the leadership. Boxer and Clover would harness themselves to the cutter or the horse-rake (no bits or reins were needed in these days, of course) and tramp steadily round and round the field with a pig walking behind and calling out "Gee up, comrade!" or "Whoa back, comrade!" as the case might be. And every animal down to the humblest worked at turning the hay and gathering it. Even the ducks and hens toiled to and fro all day in the sun, carrying tiny wisps of hay in their beaks. In the end they finished the harvest in two days' less time than it had usually taken Jones and his men. Moreover, it was the biggest harvest that the farm had ever seen. There was no wastage whatever; the hens and ducks with their sharp eyes had gathered up the very last stalk. And not an animal on the farm had stolen so much as a mouthful.

All through that summer the work of the farm went like clockwork. The animals were happy as they had never conceived it possible to be. Every mouthful of food was an acute positive pleasure, now that it was truly their own food, produced by themselves and for themselves, not doled out to them by a grudging master. With the worthless parasitical human beings gone, there was more for everyone to eat. There was more leisure too, inexperienced though the animals were. They met with many difficulties—for instance, later in the year, when they harvested the corn, they had to tread it out in the ancient style and blow away the chaff with their breath, since the farm possessed no threshing machine—but the pigs with their cleverness and Boxer with his tremendous muscles always pulled them through. Boxer was the admiration of everybody. He had been a hard worker even in Jones's time, but now he seemed more like three horses than one; there were days when the entire work of the farm seemed to rest on his mighty shoulders. From morning to night he was pushing and pulling, always at the spot where the work was hardest. He had made an arrangement with one of the cockerels to call him in the mornings half an hour earlier than anyone else, and would put in some volunteer labour at whatever seemed to be most needed, before the regular day's work began. His answer to every problem, every setback, was "I will work harder!"—which he had adopted as his personal motto.

But everyone worked according to his capacity The hens and ducks, for instance, saved five bushels of corn at the harvest by gathering up the stray grains. Nobody stole, nobody grumbled over his rations, the quarrelling and biting and jealousy which had been normal features of life in the old days had almost disappeared. Nobody shirked—or almost nobody. Mollie, it was true, was not good at getting up in the mornings, and had a way of leaving work early on the ground that there was a stone in her hoof. And the behaviour of the cat was somewhat peculiar. It was soon noticed that when there was work to be done the cat could never be found. She would vanish for hours on end, and then reappear at meal-times, or in the evening after work was over, as though nothing had happened. But she always made such excellent excuses, and purred so affectionately, that it was impossible not to believe in her good intentions. Old Benjamin, the donkey, seemed quite unchanged since the Rebellion. He did his work in the same slow obstinate way as he had done it in Jones's time, never shirking and never volunteering for extra work either. About the Rebellion and its results he would express no opinion. When asked whether he was not happier now that Jones was gone, he would say only "Donkeys live a long time. None of you has ever seen a dead donkey," and the others had to be content with this cryptic answer.

On Sundays there was no work. Breakfast was an hour later than usual, and after breakfast there was a ceremony which was observed every week without fail. First came the hoisting of the flag. Snowball had found in the harness-room an old green tablecloth of Mrs. Jones's and had painted on it a hoof and a horn in white. This was run up the flagstaff in the farmhouse garden every Sunday morning. The flag was green, Snowball explained, to represent the green fields of England, while the hoof and horn signified the future Republic of the Animals which would arise when the human race had been finally overthrown. After the hoisting of the flag all the animals trooped into the big barn for a general assembly which was known as the Meeting. Here the work of the coming week was planned out and resolutions were put forward and debated. It was always the pigs who put forward the resolutions. The other animals understood how to vote, but could never think of any resolutions of their own. Snowball and Napoleon were by far the most active in the debates. But it was noticed that these two were never in agreement: whatever suggestion either of them made, the other could be counted on to oppose it. Even when it was resolved—a thing no one could object to in itself—to set aside the small paddock behind the orchard as a home of rest for animals who were past work, there was a stormy debate over the correct retiring age for each class of animal. The Meeting always ended with the singing of *Beasts of England*, and the afternoon was given up to recreation.

The pigs had set aside the harness-room as a headquarters for themselves. Here, in the evenings, they studied blacksmithing, carpentering, and other necessary arts from books which they had brought out of the farmhouse. Snowball also busied himself with organising the other animals into what he called Animal Committees. He was indefatigable at this. He formed the Egg Production Committee for the hens, the Clean Tails League for the cows, the Wild Comrades' Re-education Committee (the object of this was to tame the rats and rabbits), the Whiter Wool Movement for the sheep, and various others, besides instituting classes in reading and writing. On the whole, these projects were a failure. The attempt to tame the wild creatures, for instance, broke down almost immediately. They continued to behave very much as before, and when treated with generosity, simply took advantage of it. The cat joined the Re-education Committee and was very active in it for some days. She was seen one day sitting on a roof and talking to some sparrows who were just out of her reach. She was telling them that all animals were now comrades and that any sparrow who chose could come and perch on her paw; but the sparrows kept their distance.

The reading and writing classes, however, were a great success. By the autumn almost every animal on the farm was literate in some degree.

As for the pigs, they could already read and write perfectly. The dogs learned to read fairly well, but were not interested in reading anything except the Seven Commandments. Muriel, the goat, could read somewhat better than the dogs, and sometimes used to read to the others in the evenings from scraps of newspaper which she found on the rubbish heap. Benjamin could read as well as any pig, but never exercised his faculty. So far as he knew, he said, there was nothing worth reading. Clover learnt the whole alphabet, but could not put words together. Boxer could not get beyond the letter D. He would trace out A, B, C, D, in the dust with his great hoof, and then would stand staring at the letters with his ears back, sometimes shaking his forelock, trying with all his might to remember what came next and never succeeding. On several occasions, indeed, he did learn E, F, G, H, but by the time he knew them, it was always discovered that he had forgotten A, B, C, and D. Finally he decided to be content with the first four letters, and used to write them out once or twice every day to refresh his memory. Mollie refused to learn any but the six letters which spelt her own name. She would form these very neatly out of pieces of twig, and would then decorate them with a flower or two and walk round them admiring them.

None of the other animals on the farm could get further than the letter A. It was also found that the stupider animals, such as the sheep, hens, and ducks, were unable to learn the Seven Commandments by heart. After much thought Snowball declared that the Seven Commandments could in effect be reduced to a single maxim, namely: "Four legs good, two legs bad." This, he said, contained the essential principle of Animalism. Whoever had thoroughly grasped it would be safe from human influences. The birds at first objected, since it seemed to them that they also had two legs, but Snowball proved to them that this was not so.

"A bird's wing, comrades," he said, "is an organ of propulsion and not of manipulation. It should therefore be regarded as a leg. The distinguishing mark of man is the *hand*, the instrument with which he does all his mischief."

The birds did not understand Snowball's long words, but they accepted his explanation, and all the humbler animals set to work to learn the new maxim by heart. FOUR LEGS GOOD, TWO LEGS BAD was inscribed on the end wall of the barn, above the Seven Commandments and in bigger letters When they had once got it by heart, the sheep developed a great liking for this maxim, and often as they lay in the field they would all start bleating "Four legs good, two legs bad! Four legs good, two legs bad!" and keep it up for hours on end, never growing tired of it.

Napoleon took no interest in Snowball's committees. He said that the education of the young was more important than anything that could be done for those who were already grown up. It happened that Jessie and Bluebell had both whelped soon after the hay harvest, giving birth between them to nine sturdy puppies. As soon as they were weaned, Napoleon took them away from their mothers, saying that he would make himself responsible for their education. He took them up into a loft which could only be reached by a ladder from the harness-room, and there kept them in such seclusion that the rest of the farm soon forgot their existence.

The mystery of where the milk went to was soon cleared up. It was mixed every day into the pigs' mash. The early apples were now ripening, and the grass of the orchard was littered with windfalls. The animals had assumed as a matter of course that these would be shared out equally; one day, however, the order went forth that all the windfalls were to be collected and brought to the harness-room for the use of the pigs. At this some of the other animals murmured, but it was no use. All the pigs were in full agreement on this point, even Snowball and Napoleon. Squealer was sent to make the necessary explanations to the others.

"Comrades!" he cried. "You do not imagine, I hope, that we pigs are doing this in a spirit of selfishness and privilege? Many of us actually dislike milk and apples. I dislike them myself. Our sole object in taking these things is to preserve our health. Milk and apples (this has been proved by Science, comrades) contain substances absolutely necessary to the well-being of a pig. We pigs are brainworkers. The whole management and organisation of this farm depend on us. Day and night we are watching over your welfare. It is for your sake that we drink that milk and eat those apples. Do you know what would happen if we pigs failed in our duty? Jones would come back! Yes, Jones would come back! Surely, comrades," cried Squealer almost pleadingly, skipping from side to side and whisking his tail, "surely there is no one among you who wants to see Jones come back?"

Now if there was one thing that the animals were completely certain of, it was that they did not want Jones back. When it was put to them in this light, they had no more to say. The importance of keeping the pigs in good health was all too obvious. So it was agreed without further argument that the milk and the windfall apples (and also the main crop of apples when they ripened) should be reserved for the pigs alone.

Chapter IV

By the late summer the news of what had happened on Animal Farm had spread across half the county. Every day Snowball and Napoleon sent out flights of pigeons whose instructions were to mingle with the animals on neighbouring farms, tell them the story of the Rebellion, and teach them the tune of *Beasts of England.*

Most of this time Mr. Jones had spent sitting in the taproom of the Red Lion at Willingdon, complaining to anyone who would listen of the monstrous injustice he had suffered in being turned out of his property by a pack of good-for-nothing animals. The other farmers sympathised in principle, but they did not at first give him much help. At heart, each of them was secretly wondering whether he could not somehow turn Jones's misfortune to his own advantage. It was lucky that the owners of the two farms which adjoined Animal Farm were on permanently bad terms. One of them, which was named Foxwood, was a large, neglected, old-fashioned farm, much overgrown by woodland, with all its pastures worn out and its hedges in a disgraceful condition. Its owner, Mr. Pilkington, was an easy-going gentleman farmer who spent most of his time in fishing or hunting according to the season. The other farm, which was called Pinchfield, was smaller and better kept. Its owner was a Mr. Frederick, a tough, shrewd man, perpetually involved in lawsuits and with a name for driving hard bargains. These two disliked each other so much that it was difficult for them to come to any agreement, even in defence of their own interests.

Nevertheless, they were both thoroughly frightened by the rebellion on Animal Farm, and very anxious to prevent their own animals from learning too much about it. At first they pretended to laugh to scorn the idea of animals managing a farm for themselves. The whole thing would be over in a fortnight, they said. They put it about that the animals on the Manor Farm (they insisted on calling it the Manor Farm; they would not tolerate the name "Animal Farm") were perpetually fighting among themselves and were also rapidly starving to death. When time passed and the animals had evidently not starved to death, Frederick and Pilkington changed their tune and began to talk of the terrible wickedness that now flourished on Animal Farm. It was given out that the animals there practised cannibalism, tortured one another with red-hot horseshoes, and had their females in common. This was what came of rebelling against the laws of Nature, Frederick and Pilkington said.

However, these stories were never fully believed. Rumours of a wonderful farm, where the human beings had been turned out and the animals managed their own affairs, continued to circulate in vague and distorted forms, and throughout that year a wave of rebelliousness ran through the countryside. Bulls which had always been tractable suddenly turned savage, sheep broke down hedges and devoured the clover, cows kicked the pail over, hunters refused their fences and shot their riders on to the other side. Above all, the tune and even the words of *Beasts of England* were known everywhere. It had spread with astonishing speed. The human beings could not contain their rage when they heard this song, though they pretended to think it merely ridiculous. They could not understand, they said, how even animals could bring themselves to sing such contemptible rubbish. Any animal caught singing it was given a flogging on the spot. And yet the song was irrepressible. The blackbirds whistled it in the hedges, the pigeons cooed it in the elms, it got into the din of the smithies and the tune of the church bells. And when the human beings listened to it, they secretly trembled, hearing in it a prophecy of their future doom.

Early in October, when the corn was cut and stacked and some of it was already threshed, a flight of pigeons came whirling through the air and alighted in the yard of Animal Farm in the wildest excitement. Jones and all his men, with half a dozen others from Foxwood and Pinchfield, had entered the five-barred gate and were coming up the cart-track that led to the farm. They were all carrying sticks, except Jones, who was marching ahead with a gun in his hands. Obviously they were going to attempt the recapture of the farm.

This had long been expected, and all preparations had been made. Snowball, who had studied an old book of Julius Caesar's campaigns which he had found in the farmhouse, was in charge of the defensive operations. He gave his orders quickly, and in a couple of minutes every animal was at his post.

As the human beings approached the farm buildings, Snowball launched his first attack. All the pigeons, to the number of thirty-five, flew to and fro over the men's heads and muted upon them from mid-air; and while the men were dealing with this, the geese, who had been hiding behind the hedge, rushed out and pecked viciously at the calves of their legs. However, this was only a light skirmishing manoeuvre, intended to create a little disorder, and the men easily drove the geese off with their sticks. Snowball now launched his second line of attack. Muriel, Benjamin, and all the sheep, with Snowball at the head of them, rushed forward and prodded and butted the men from every side, while Benjamin turned around and lashed at them with his small hoofs. But once again the men, with their sticks and their hobnailed boots, were too strong for them; and suddenly, at a squeal from Snowball, which was the signal for retreat, all the animals turned and fled through the gateway into the yard.

The men gave a shout of triumph. They saw, as they imagined, their enemies in flight, and they rushed after them in disorder. This was just what Snowball had intended. As soon as they were well inside the yard, the three horses, the three cows, and the rest of the pigs, who had been lying in ambush in the cowshed, suddenly emerged in their rear, cutting them off. Snowball now gave the signal for the charge. He himself dashed straight for Jones. Jones saw him coming, raised his gun and fired. The pellets scored bloody streaks along Snowball's back, and a sheep dropped dead. Without halting for an instant, Snowball flung his fifteen stone against Jones's legs. Jones was hurled into a pile of dung and his gun flew out of his hands. But the most terrifying spectacle of all was Boxer, rearing up on his hind legs and striking out with his great iron-shod hoofs like a stallion. His very first blow took a stable-lad from Foxwood on the skull and stretched him lifeless in the mud. At the sight, several men dropped their sticks and tried to run. Panic overtook them, and the next moment all the animals together were chasing them round and round the yard. They were gored, kicked, bitten, trampled on. There was not an animal on the farm that did not take vengeance on them after his own fashion. Even the cat suddenly leapt off a roof onto a cowman's shoulders and sank her claws in his neck, at which he yelled horribly. At a moment when the opening was clear, the men were glad enough to rush out of the yard and make a bolt for the main road. And so within five minutes of their invasion they were in ignominious retreat by the same way as they had come, with a flock of geese hissing after them and pecking at their calves all the way.

All the men were gone except one. Back in the yard Boxer was pawing with his hoof at the stable-lad who lay face down in the mud, trying to turn him over. The boy did not stir.

"He is dead," said Boxer sorrowfully. "I had no intention of doing that. I forgot that I was wearing iron shoes. Who will believe that I did not do this on purpose?"

"No sentimentality, comrade!" cried Snowball from whose wounds the blood was still dripping. "War is war. The only good human being is a dead one."

"I have no wish to take life, not even human life," repeated Boxer, and his eyes were full of tears.

"Where is Mollie?" exclaimed somebody.

Mollie in fact was missing. For a moment there was great alarm; it was feared that the men might have harmed her in some way, or even carried her off with them. In the end, however, she was found hiding in her stall with her head buried among the hay in the manger. She had taken to flight as soon as the gun went off. And when the others came back from looking for her, it was to find that the stable-lad, who in fact was only stunned, had already recovered and made off.

The animals had now reassembled in the wildest excitement, each recounting his own exploits in the battle at the top of his voice. An impromptu celebration of the victory was held immediately. The flag was run up and *Beasts of England* was sung a number of times, then the sheep who had been killed was given a solemn funeral, a hawthorn bush being planted on her grave. At the graveside Snowball made a little speech, emphasising the need for all animals to be ready to die for Animal Farm if need be.

The animals decided unanimously to create a military decoration, "Animal Hero, First Class," which was conferred there and then on Snowball and Boxer. It consisted of a brass medal (they were really some old horse-brasses which had been found in the harness-room), to be worn on Sundays and holidays. There was also "Animal Hero, Second Class," which was conferred posthumously on the dead sheep.

There was much discussion as to what the battle should be called. In the end, it was named the Battle of the Cowshed, since that was where the ambush had been sprung. Mr. Jones's gun had been found lying in the mud, and it was known that there was a supply of cartridges in the farmhouse. It was decided to set the gun up at the foot of the flagstaff, like a piece of artillery, and to fire it twice a year—once on October the twelfth, the anniversary of the Battle of the Cowshed, and once on Midsummer Day, the anniversary of the Rebellion.

Chapter V

As winter drew on, Mollie became more and more troublesome. She was late for work every morning and excused herself by saying that she had overslept, and she complained of mysterious pains, although her appetite was excellent. On every kind of pretext she would run away from work and go to the drinking pool, where she would stand foolishly gazing at her own reflection in the water. But there were also rumours of something more serious. One day, as Mollie strolled blithely into the yard, flirting her long tail and chewing at a stalk of hay, Clover took her aside.

"Mollie," she said, "I have something very serious to say to you. This morning I saw you looking over the hedge that divides Animal Farm from Foxwood. One of Mr. Pilkington's men was standing on the other side of the hedge. And—I was a long way away, but I am almost certain I saw this—he was talking to you and you were allowing him to stroke your nose. What does that mean, Mollie?"

"He didn't! I wasn't! It isn't true!" cried Mollie, beginning to prance about and paw the ground.

"Mollie! Look me in the face. Do you give me your word of honour that that man was not stroking your nose?"

"It isn't true!" repeated Mollie, but she could not look Clover in the face, and the next moment she took to her heels and galloped away into the field.

A thought struck Clover. Without saying anything to the others, she went to Mollie's stall and turned over the straw with her hoof. Hidden under the straw was a little pile of lump sugar and several bunches of ribbon of different colours.

Three days later Mollie disappeared. For some weeks nothing was known of her whereabouts, then the pigeons reported that they had seen her on the other side of Willingdon. She was between the shafts of a smart dogcart painted red and black, which was standing outside a public-house. A fat red-faced man in check breeches and gaiters, who looked like a publican, was stroking her nose and feeding her with sugar. Her coat was newly clipped and she wore a scarlet ribbon round her forelock. She appeared to be enjoying herself, so the pigeons said. None of the animals ever mentioned Mollie again.

In January there came bitterly hard weather. The earth was like iron, and nothing could be done in the fields. Many meetings were held in the big barn, and the pigs occupied themselves with planning out the work of the coming season. It had come to be accepted that the pigs, who were manifestly cleverer than the other animals, should decide all questions of farm policy, though their decisions had to be ratified by a majority vote. This arrangement would have worked well enough if it had not been for the disputes between Snowball and Napoleon. These two disagreed at every point where disagreement was possible. If one of them suggested sowing a bigger acreage with barley, the other was certain to demand a bigger acreage of oats, and if one of them said that such and such a field was just right for cabbages, the other would declare that it was useless for anything except roots.

Each had his own following, and there were some violent debates. At the Meetings Snowball often won over the majority by his brilliant speeches, but Napoleon was better at canvassing support for himself in between times. He was especially successful with the sheep. Of late the sheep had taken to bleating "Four legs good, two legs bad" both in and out of season, and they often interrupted the Meeting with this. It was noticed that they were especially liable to break into "Four legs good, two legs bad" at crucial moments in Snowball's speeches. Snowball had made a close study of some back numbers of the *Farmer and Stockbreeder* which he had found in the farmhouse, and was full of plans for innovations and improvements. He talked learnedly about field drains, silage, and basic slag, and had worked out a complicated scheme for all the animals to drop their dung directly in the fields, at a different spot every day, to save the labour of cartage. Napoleon produced no schemes of his own, but said quietly that Snowball's would come to nothing, and seemed to be biding his time. But of all their controversies, none was so bitter as the one that took place over the windmill.

In the long pasture, not far from the farm buildings, there was a small knoll which was the highest point on the farm. After surveying the ground, Snowball declared that this was just the place for a windmill, which could be made to operate a dynamo and supply the farm with electrical power. This would light the stalls and warm them in winter, and would also run a circular saw, a chaff-cutter, a mangel-slicer, and an electric milking machine. The animals had never heard of anything of this kind before (for the farm was an old-fashioned one and had only the most primitive machinery), and they listened in astonishment while Snowball conjured up pictures of fantastic machines which would do their work for them while they grazed at their ease in the fields or improved their minds with reading and conversation.

Within a few weeks Snowball's plans for the windmill were fully worked out. The mechanical details came mostly from three books which had belonged to Mr. Jones—*One Thousand Useful Things to Do About the House, Every Man His Own Bricklayer,* and *Electricity for Beginners*. Snowball used as his study a shed which had once been used for incubators and had a smooth wooden floor, suitable for drawing on. He was closeted there for hours at a time. With his books held open by a stone, and with a piece of chalk gripped between the knuckles of his trotter, he would move rapidly to and fro, drawing in line after line and uttering little whimpers of excitement. Gradually the plans grew into a complicated mass of cranks and cog-wheels, covering more than half the floor, which the other animals found completely unintelligible but very impressive. All of them came to look at Snowball's drawings at least once a day. Even the hens and ducks came, and were at pains not to tread on the chalk marks. Only Napoleon held aloof. He had declared himself against the windmill from the start. One day, however, he arrived unexpectedly to examine the plans. He walked heavily round the shed, looked closely at every detail of the plans and snuffed at them once or twice, then stood for a little while contemplating them out of the corner of his eye; then suddenly he lifted his leg, urinated over the plans, and walked out without uttering a word.

The whole farm was deeply divided on the subject of the windmill. Snowball did not deny that to build it would be a difficult business. Stone would have to be carried and built up into walls, then the sails would have to be made and after that there would be need for dynamos and cables. (How these were to be procured, Snowball did not say.) But he maintained that it could all be done in a year. And thereafter, he declared, so much labour would be saved that the animals would only need to work three days a week. Napoleon, on the other hand, argued that the great need of the moment was to increase food production, and that if they wasted time on the windmill they would all starve to death. The animals formed themselves into two factions under the slogan, "Vote for Snowball and the three-day week" and "Vote for Napoleon and the full manger." Benjamin was the only animal who did not side with either faction. He refused to believe either that food would become more plentiful or that the windmill would save work. Windmill or no windmill, he said, life would go on as it had always gone on—that is, badly.

Apart from the disputes over the windmill, there was the question of the defence of the farm. It was fully realised that though the human beings had been defeated in the Battle of the Cowshed they might make another and more determined attempt to recapture the farm and reinstate Mr. Jones. They had all the more reason for doing so because the news of their defeat had spread across the countryside and made the animals on the neighbouring farms more restive than ever. As usual, Snowball and Napoleon were in disagreement. According to Napoleon, what the animals must do was to procure firearms and train themselves in the use of them.

According to Snowball, they must send out more and more pigeons and stir up rebellion among the animals on the other farms. The one argued that if they could not defend themselves they were bound to be conquered, the other argued that if rebellions happened everywhere they would have no need to defend themselves. The animals listened first to Napoleon, then to Snowball, and could not make up their minds which was right; indeed, they always found themselves in agreement with the one who was speaking at the moment.

At last the day came when Snowball's plans were completed. At the Meeting on the following Sunday the question of whether or not to begin work on the windmill was to be put to the vote. When the animals had assembled in the big barn, Snowball stood up and, though occasionally interrupted by bleating from the sheep, set forth his reasons for advocating the building of the windmill. Then Napoleon stood up to reply. He said very quietly that the windmill was nonsense and that he advised nobody to vote for it, and promptly sat down again; he had spoken for barely thirty seconds, and seemed almost indifferent as to the effect he produced. At this Snowball sprang to his feet, and shouting down the sheep, who had begun bleating again, broke into a passionate appeal in favour of the windmill. Until now the animals had been about equally divided in their sympathies, but in a moment Snowball's eloquence had carried them away. In glowing sentences he painted a picture of Animal Farm as it might be when sordid labour was lifted from the animals' backs. His imagination had now run far beyond chaff-cutters and turnip-slicers. Electricity, he said, could operate threshing machines, ploughs, harrows, rollers, and reapers and binders, besides supplying every stall with its own electric light, hot and cold water, and an electric heater. By the time he had finished speaking, there was no doubt as to which way the vote would go. But just at this moment Napoleon stood up and, casting a peculiar sidelong look at Snowball, uttered a high-pitched whimper of a kind no one had ever heard him utter before.

At this there was a terrible baying sound outside, and nine enormous dogs wearing brass-studded collars came bounding into the barn. They dashed straight for Snowball, who only sprang from his place just in time to escape their snapping jaws. In a moment he was out of the door and they were after him. Too amazed and frightened to speak, all the animals crowded through the door to watch the chase. Snowball was racing across the long pasture that led to the road. He was running as only a pig can run, but the dogs were close on his heels. Suddenly he slipped and it seemed certain that they had him. Then he was up again, running faster than ever, then the dogs were gaining on him again. One of them all but closed his jaws on Snowball's tail, but Snowball whisked it free just in time. Then he put on an extra spurt and, with a few inches to spare, slipped through a hole in the hedge and was seen no more.

Silent and terrified, the animals crept back into the barn. In a moment the dogs came bounding back. At first no one had been able to imagine where these creatures came from, but the problem was soon solved: they were the puppies whom Napoleon had taken away from their mothers and reared privately. Though not yet full-grown, they were huge dogs, and as fierce-looking as wolves. They kept close to

Napoleon. It was noticed that they wagged their tails to him in the same way as the other dogs had been used to do to Mr. Jones.

Napoleon, with the dogs following him, now mounted on to the raised portion of the floor where Major had previously stood to deliver his speech. He announced that from now on the Sunday-morning Meetings would come to an end. They were unnecessary, he said, and wasted time. In future all questions relating to the working of the farm would be settled by a special committee of pigs, presided over by himself. These would meet in private and afterwards communicate their decisions to the others. The animals would still assemble on Sunday mornings to salute the flag, sing *Beasts of England*, and receive their orders for the week; but there would be no more debates.

In spite of the shock that Snowball's expulsion had given them, the animals were dismayed by this announcement. Several of them would have protested if they could have found the right arguments. Even Boxer was vaguely troubled. He set his ears back, shook his forelock several times, and tried hard to marshal his thoughts; but in the end he could not think of anything to say. Some of the pigs themselves, however, were more articulate. Four young porkers in the front row uttered shrill squeals of disapproval, and all four of them sprang to their feet and began speaking at once. But suddenly the dogs sitting round Napoleon let out deep, menacing growls, and the pigs fell silent and sat down again. Then the sheep broke out into a tremendous bleating of "Four legs good, two legs bad!" which went on for nearly a quarter of an hour and put an end to any chance of discussion.

Afterwards Squealer was sent round the farm to explain the new arrangement to the others.

"Comrades," he said, "I trust that every animal here appreciates the sacrifice that Comrade Napoleon has made in taking this extra labour upon himself. Do not imagine, comrades, that leadership is a pleasure! On the contrary, it is a deep and heavy responsibility. No one believes more firmly than Comrade Napoleon that all animals are equal. He would be only too happy to let you make your decisions for yourselves. But sometimes you might make the wrong decisions, comrades, and then where should we be? Suppose you had decided to follow Snowball, with his moonshine of windmills—Snowball, who, as we now know, was no better than a criminal?"

"He fought bravely at the Battle of the Cowshed," said somebody.

"Bravery is not enough," said Squealer. "Loyalty and obedience are more important. And as to the Battle of the Cowshed, I believe the time will come when we shall find that Snowball's part in it was much exaggerated. Discipline, comrades, iron discipline! That is the watchword for today. One false step, and our enemies would be upon us. Surely, comrades, you do not want Jones back?"

Once again this argument was unanswerable. Certainly the animals did not want Jones back; if the holding of debates on Sunday mornings was liable to bring him back, then the debates must stop. Boxer, who had now had time to think things over, voiced the general feeling by saying: "If Comrade Napoleon says it, it must be right." And from then on he adopted the maxim, "Napoleon is always right," in addition to his private motto of "I will work harder."

By this time the weather had broken and the spring ploughing had begun. The shed where Snowball had drawn his plans of the windmill had been shut up and it was assumed that the plans had been rubbed off the floor. Every Sunday morning at ten o'clock the animals assembled in the big barn to receive their orders for the week. The skull of old Major, now clean of flesh, had been disinterred from the orchard and set up on a stump at the foot of the flagstaff, beside the gun. After the hoisting of the flag, the animals were required to file past the skull in a reverent manner before entering the barn. Nowadays they did not sit all together as they had done in the past. Napoleon, with Squealer and another pig named Minimus, who had a remarkable gift for composing songs and poems, sat on the front of the raised platform, with the nine young dogs forming a semicircle round them, and the other pigs sitting behind. The rest of the animals sat facing them in the main body of the barn. Napoleon read out the orders for the week in a gruff soldierly style, and after a single singing of *Beasts of England,* all the animals dispersed.

On the third Sunday after Snowball's expulsion, the animals were somewhat surprised to hear Napoleon announce that the windmill was to be built after all. He did not give any reason for having changed his mind, but merely warned the animals that this extra task would mean very hard work, it might even be necessary to reduce their rations. The plans, however, had all been prepared, down to the last detail. A special committee of pigs had been at work upon them for the past three weeks. The building of the windmill, with various other improvements, was expected to take two years.

That evening Squealer explained privately to the other animals that Napoleon had never in reality been opposed to the windmill. On the contrary, it was he who had advocated it in the beginning, and the plan which Snowball had drawn on the floor of the incubator shed had actually been stolen from among Napoleon's papers. The windmill was, in fact, Napoleon's own creation. Why, then, asked somebody, had he spoken so strongly against it? Here Squealer looked very sly. That, he said, was Comrade Napoleon's cunning. He had *seemed* to oppose the windmill, simply as a manoeuvre to get rid of Snowball, who was a dangerous character and a bad influence. Now that Snowball was out of the way, the plan could go forward without his interference. This, said Squealer, was something called tactics. He repeated a number of times, "Tactics, comrades, tactics!" skipping round and whisking his tail with a merry laugh. The animals were not certain what the word meant, but Squealer spoke so persuasively, and the three dogs who happened to be with him growled so threateningly, that they accepted his explanation without further questions.

Chapter VI

All that year the animals worked like slaves. But they were happy in their work; they grudged no effort or sacrifice, well aware that everything that they did was for the benefit of themselves and those of their kind who would come after them, and not for a pack of idle, thieving human beings.

Throughout the spring and summer they worked a sixty-hour week, and in August Napoleon announced that there would be work on Sunday afternoons as well. This work was strictly voluntary, but any animal who absented himself from it would have his rations reduced by half. Even so, it was found necessary to leave certain tasks undone. The harvest was a little less successful than in the previous year, and two fields which should have been sown with roots in the early summer were not sown because the ploughing had not been completed early enough. It was possible to foresee that the coming winter would be a hard one.

The windmill presented unexpected difficulties. There was a good quarry of limestone on the farm, and plenty of sand and cement had been found in one of the outhouses, so that all the materials for building were at hand. But the problem the animals could not at first solve was how to break up the stone into pieces of suitable size. There seemed no way of doing this except with picks and crowbars, which no animal could use, because no animal could stand on his hind legs. Only after weeks of vain effort did the right idea occur to somebody—namely, to utilise the force of gravity. Huge boulders, far too big to be used as they were, were lying all over the bed of the quarry. The animals lashed ropes round these, and then all together, cows, horses, sheep, any animal that could lay hold of the rope—even the pigs sometimes joined in at critical moments—they dragged them with desperate slowness up the slope to the top of the quarry, where they were toppled over the edge, to shatter to pieces below. Transporting the stone when it was once broken was comparatively simple. The horses carried it off in cart-loads, the sheep dragged single blocks, even Muriel and Benjamin yoked themselves into an old governess-cart and did their share. By late summer a sufficient store of stone had accumulated, and then the building began, under the superintendence of the pigs.

But it was a slow, laborious process. Frequently it took a whole day of exhausting effort to drag a single boulder to the top of the quarry, and sometimes when it was pushed over the edge it failed to break. Nothing could have been achieved without Boxer, whose strength seemed equal to that of all the rest of the animals put together. When the boulder began to slip and the animals cried out in despair at finding themselves dragged down the hill, it was always Boxer who strained himself against the rope and brought the boulder to a stop. To see him toiling up the slope inch by inch, his breath coming fast, the tips of his hoofs clawing at the ground, and his great sides matted with sweat, filled everyone with admiration. Clover warned him sometimes to be careful not to overstrain himself, but Boxer would never listen to her. His two slogans, "I will work harder" and "Napoleon is always right," seemed to him a sufficient answer to all problems. He had made arrangements with the cockerel to call him three-quarters of an hour earlier in the mornings instead of half an hour. And in his spare moments, of which there were not many nowadays, he would go alone to the quarry, collect a load of broken stone, and drag it down to the site of the windmill unassisted.

The animals were not badly off throughout that summer, in spite of the hardness of their work. If they had no more food than they had had in Jones's day, at least they did not have less. The advantage of only having to feed themselves, and not having to support five extravagant human beings as well, was so great that it would have taken a lot of failures to outweigh it. And in many ways the animal method of doing things was more efficient and saved labour. Such jobs as weeding, for instance, could be done with a thoroughness impossible to human beings. And again, since no animal now stole, it was unnecessary to fence off pasture from arable land, which saved a lot of labour on the upkeep of hedges and gates. Nevertheless, as the summer wore on, various unforeseen shortages began to make them selves felt. There was need of paraffin oil, nails, string, dog biscuits, and iron for the horses' shoes, none of which could be produced on the farm. Later there would also be need for seeds and artificial manures, besides various tools and, finally, the machinery for the windmill. How these were to be procured, no one was able to imagine.

One Sunday morning, when the animals assembled to receive their orders, Napoleon announced that he had decided upon a new policy. From now onwards Animal Farm would engage in trade with the neighbouring farms: not, of course, for any commercial purpose, but simply in order to obtain certain materials which were urgently necessary. The needs of the windmill must override everything else, he said. He was therefore making arrangements to sell a stack of hay and part of the current year's wheat crop, and later on, if more money were needed, it would have to be made up by the sale of eggs, for which there was always a market in Willingdon. The hens, said Napoleon, should welcome this sacrifice as their own special contribution towards the building of the windmill.

Once again the animals were conscious of a vague uneasiness. Never to have any dealings with human beings, never to engage in trade, never to make use of money—had not these been among the earliest resolutions passed at that first triumphant Meeting after Jones was expelled? All the animals remembered passing such resolutions: or at least they thought that they remembered it. The four young pigs who had protested when Napoleon abolished the Meetings raised their voices timidly, but they were promptly silenced by a tremendous growling from the dogs. Then, as usual, the sheep broke into "Four legs good, two legs bad!" and the momentary awkwardness was smoothed over. Finally Napoleon raised his trotter for silence and announced that he had already made all the arrangements. There would be no need for any of the animals to come in contact with human beings, which would clearly be most undesirable. He intended to take the whole burden upon his own shoulders. A Mr.

Whymper, a solicitor living in Willingdon, had agreed to act as intermediary between Animal Farm and the outside world, and would visit the farm every Monday morning to receive his instructions. Napoleon ended his speech with his usual cry of "Long live Animal Farm!" and after the singing of *Beasts of England* the animals were dismissed.

Afterwards Squealer made a round of the farm and set the animals' minds at rest. He assured them that the resolution against engaging in trade and using money had never been passed, or even suggested. It was pure imagination, probably traceable in the beginning to lies circulated by Snowball. A few animals still felt faintly doubtful, but Squealer asked them shrewdly, "Are you certain that this is not something that you have dreamed, comrades? Have you any record of such a resolution? Is it written down anywhere?" And since it was certainly true that nothing of the kind existed in writing, the animals were satisfied that they had been mistaken.

Every Monday Mr. Whymper visited the farm as had been arranged. He was a sly-looking little man with side whiskers, a solicitor in a very small way of business, but sharp enough to have realised earlier than anyone else that Animal Farm would need a broker and that the commissions would be worth having. The animals watched his coming and going with a kind of dread, and avoided him as much as possible. Nevertheless, the sight of Napoleon, on all fours, delivering orders to Whymper, who stood on two legs, roused their pride and partly reconciled them to the new arrangement. Their relations with the human race were now not quite the same as they had been before. The human beings did not hate Animal Farm any less now that it was prospering; indeed, they hated it more than ever. Every human being held it as an article of faith that the farm would go bankrupt sooner or later, and, above all, that the windmill would be a failure. They would meet in the public-houses and prove to one another by means of diagrams that the windmill was bound to fall down, or that if it did stand up, then that it would never work. And yet, against their will, they had developed a certain respect for the efficiency with which the animals were managing their own affairs. One symptom of this was that they had begun to call Animal Farm by its proper name and ceased to pretend that it was called the Manor Farm. They had also dropped their championship of Jones, who had given up hope of getting his farm back and gone to live in another part of the country. Except through Whymper, there was as yet no contact between Animal Farm and the outside world, but there were constant rumours that Napoleon was about to enter into a definite business agreement either with Mr. Pilkington of Foxwood or with Mr. Frederick of Pinchfield—but never, it was noticed, with both simultaneously.

It was about this time that the pigs suddenly moved into the farmhouse and took up their residence there. Again the animals seemed to remember that a resolution against this had been passed in the early days, and again Squealer was able to convince them that this was not the case. It was absolutely necessary, he said, that the pigs, who were the brains of the farm, should have a quiet place to work in. It was also more suited to the dignity of the Leader (for of late he had taken to speaking of Napoleon under the title of "Leader") to live in a house than in a mere sty. Nevertheless, some of the animals were disturbed when they heard that the pigs not only took their meals in the kitchen and used the drawing-room as a recreation room, but also slept in the beds. Boxer passed it off as usual with "Napoleon is always right!", but Clover, who thought she remembered a definite ruling against beds, went to the end of the barn and tried to puzzle out the Seven Commandments which were inscribed there. Finding herself unable to read more than individual letters, she fetched Muriel.

"Muriel," she said, "read me the Fourth Commandment. Does it not say something about never sleeping in a bed?"

With some difficulty Muriel spelt it out.

"It says, 'No animal shall sleep in a bed *with sheets*,'" she announced finally.

Curiously enough, Clover had not remembered that the Fourth Commandment mentioned sheets; but as it was there on the wall, it must have done so. And Squealer, who happened to be passing at this moment, attended by two or three dogs, was able to put the whole matter in its proper perspective.

"You have heard then, comrades," he said, "that we pigs now sleep in the beds of the farmhouse? And why not? You did not suppose, surely, that there was ever a ruling against *beds*? A bed merely means a place to sleep in. A pile of straw in a stall is a bed, properly regarded. The rule was against *sheets*, which are a human invention. We have removed the *sheets* from the farmhouse beds, and sleep between blankets. And very comfortable beds they are too! But not more comfortable than we need, I can tell you, comrades, with all the brainwork we have to do nowadays. You would not rob us of our repose, would you, comrades? You would not have us too tired to carry out our duties? Surely none of you wishes to see Jones back?"

The animals reassured him on this point immediately, and no more was said about the pigs sleeping in the farmhouse beds. And when, some days afterwards, it was announced that from now on the pigs would get up an hour later in the mornings than the other animals, no complaint was made about that either.

By the autumn the animals were tired but happy. They had had a hard year, and after the sale of part of the hay and corn, the stores of food for the winter were none too plentiful, but the windmill compensated for everything. It was almost half built now. After the harvest there was a stretch of clear dry weather, and the animals toiled harder than ever, thinking it well worth while to plod to and fro all day with blocks of stone if by doing so they could raise the walls another foot. Boxer would even come out at nights and work for an hour or two on his own by the light of the harvest moon. In their spare moments the animals would walk round and round the half-finished mill, admiring the strength and perpendicularity of its walls and marvelling that they should ever have been able to build anything so imposing. Only old Benjamin refused to grow enthusiastic about the windmill, though, as usual, he would utter nothing beyond the cryptic remark that donkeys live a long time.

November came, with raging south-west winds. Building had to stop because it was now too wet to mix the cement. Finally there came a night when the gale was so violent that the farm buildings rocked on their foundations and several tiles were blown off the roof of the barn. The hens woke up squawking with terror because they had all dreamed simultaneously of hearing a gun go off in the distance. In the morning the animals came out of their stalls to find that the flagstaff had been blown down and an elm tree at the foot of the orchard had been plucked up like a radish. They had just noticed this when a cry of despair broke from every animal's throat. A terrible sight had met their eyes. The windmill was in ruins.

With one accord they dashed down to the spot. Napoleon, who seldom moved out of a walk, raced ahead of them all. Yes, there it lay, the fruit of all their struggles, levelled to its foundations, the stones they had broken and carried so laboriously scattered all around. Unable at first to speak, they stood gazing mournfully at the litter of fallen stone Napoleon paced to and fro in silence, occasionally snuffing at the ground. His tail had grown rigid and twitched sharply from side to side, a sign in him of intense mental activity. Suddenly he halted as though his mind were made up.

"Comrades," he said quietly, "do you know who is responsible for this? Do you know the enemy who has come in the night and overthrown our windmill? SNOWBALL!" he suddenly roared in a voice of thunder. "Snowball has done this thing! In sheer malignity, thinking to set back our plans and avenge himself for his ignominious expulsion, this traitor has crept here under cover of night and destroyed our work of nearly a year. Comrades, here and now I pronounce the death sentence upon Snowball. 'Animal Hero, Second Class,' and half a bushel of apples to any animal who brings him to justice. A full bushel to anyone who captures him alive!"

The animals were shocked beyond measure to learn that even Snowball could be guilty of such an action. There was a cry of indignation, and everyone began thinking out ways of catching Snowball if he should ever come back. Almost immediately the footprints of a pig were discovered in the grass at a little distance from the knoll. They could only be traced for a few yards, but appeared to lead to a hole in the hedge. Napoleon snuffed deeply at them and pronounced them to be Snowball's. He gave it as his opinion that Snowball had probably come from the direction of Foxwood Farm.

"No more delays, comrades!" cried Napoleon when the footprints had been examined. "There is work to be done. This very morning we begin rebuilding the windmill, and we will build all through the winter, rain or shine. We will teach this miserable traitor that he cannot undo our work so easily. Remember, comrades, there must be no alteration in our plans: they shall be carried out to the day. Forward, comrades! Long live the windmill! Long live Animal Farm!"

Chapter VII

It was a bitter winter. The stormy weather was followed by sleet and snow, and then by a hard frost which did not break till well into February. The animals carried on as best they could with the rebuilding of the windmill, well knowing that the outside world was watching them and that the envious human beings would rejoice and triumph if the mill were not finished on time.

Out of spite, the human beings pretended not to believe that it was Snowball who had destroyed the windmill: they said that it had fallen down because the walls were too thin. The animals knew that this was not the case. Still, it had been decided to build the walls three feet thick this time instead of eighteen inches as before, which meant collecting much larger quantities of stone. For a long time the quarry was full of snowdrifts and nothing could be done. Some progress was made in the dry frosty weather that followed, but it was cruel work, and the animals could not feel so hopeful about it as they had felt before. They were always cold, and usually hungry as well. Only Boxer and Clover never lost heart. Squealer made excellent speeches on the joy of service and the dignity of labour, but the other animals found more inspiration in Boxer's strength and his never-failing cry of "I will work harder!"

In January food fell short. The corn ration was drastically reduced, and it was announced that an extra potato ration would be issued to make up for it. Then it was discovered that the greater part of the potato crop had been frosted in the clamps, which had not been covered thickly enough. The potatoes had become soft and discoloured, and only a few were edible. For days at a time the animals had nothing to eat but chaff and mangels. Starvation seemed to stare them in the face.

It was vitally necessary to conceal this fact from the outside world. Emboldened by the collapse of the windmill, the human beings were inventing fresh lies about Animal Farm. Once again it was being put about that all the animals were dying of famine and disease, and that they were continually fighting among themselves and had resorted to cannibalism and infanticide. Napoleon was well aware of the bad results that might follow if the real facts of the food situation were known, and he decided to make use of Mr. Whymper to spread a contrary impression. Hitherto the animals had had little or no contact with Whymper on his weekly visits: now, however, a few selected animals, mostly sheep, were instructed to remark casually in his hearing that rations had been increased. In addition, Napoleon ordered the almost empty bins in the store-shed to be filled nearly to the brim with sand, which was then covered up with what remained of the grain and meal. On some suitable pretext Whymper was led through the store-shed and allowed to catch a glimpse of the bins. He was deceived, and continued to report to the outside world that there was no food shortage on Animal Farm.

Nevertheless, towards the end of January it became obvious that it would be necessary to procure some more grain from somewhere. In these days Napoleon rarely appeared in public, but spent all his time in the farmhouse, which was guarded at each door by fierce-looking dogs. When he did emerge, it was in a ceremonial manner, with an escort of six dogs who closely surrounded him and growled if anyone came too near. Frequently he did not even appear on Sunday mornings, but issued his orders through one of the other pigs, usually Squealer.

One Sunday morning Squealer announced that the hens, who had just come in to lay again, must surrender their eggs. Napoleon had accepted, through Whymper, a contract for four hundred eggs a week. The price of these would pay for enough grain and meal to keep the farm going till summer came on and conditions were easier.

When the hens heard this, they raised a terrible outcry. They had been warned earlier that this sacrifice might be necessary, but had not believed that it would really happen. They were just getting their clutches ready for the spring sitting, and they protested that to take the eggs away now was murder. For the first time since the expulsion of Jones, there was something resembling a rebellion. Led by three young Black Minorca pullets, the hens made a determined effort to thwart Napoleon's wishes. Their method was to fly up to the rafters and there lay their eggs, which smashed to pieces on the floor. Napoleon acted swiftly and ruthlessly. He ordered the hens' rations to be stopped, and decreed that any animal giving so much as a grain of corn to a hen should be punished by death. The dogs saw to it that these orders were carried out. For five days the hens held out, then they capitulated and went back to their nesting boxes. Nine hens had died in the meantime. Their bodies were buried in the orchard, and it was given out that they had died of coccidiosis. Whymper heard nothing of this affair, and the eggs were duly delivered, a grocer's van driving up to the farm once a week to take them away.

All this while no more had been seen of Snowball. He was rumoured to be hiding on one of the neighbouring farms, either Foxwood or Pinchfield. Napoleon was by this time on slightly better terms with the other farmers than before. It happened that there was in the yard a pile of timber which had been stacked there ten years earlier when a beech spinney was cleared. It was well seasoned, and Whymper had advised Napoleon to sell it; both Mr. Pilkington and Mr. Frederick were anxious to buy it. Napoleon was hesitating between the two, unable to make up his mind. It was noticed that whenever he seemed on the point of coming to an agreement with Frederick, Snowball was declared to be in hiding at Foxwood, while, when he inclined toward Pilkington, Snowball was said to be at Pinchfield.

Suddenly, early in the spring, an alarming thing was discovered. Snowball was secretly frequenting the farm by night! The animals were so disturbed that they could hardly sleep in their stalls. Every night, it was said, he came creeping in under cover of darkness and performed all kinds of mischief. He stole the corn, he upset the milk-pails, he broke the eggs, he trampled the seedbeds, he gnawed the bark off the fruit trees. Whenever anything went wrong it became usual to attribute it to Snowball. If a window was broken or a drain was blocked up, someone was certain to say that Snowball had come in the night and done it, and when the key of the store-shed was lost, the whole farm was convinced that Snowball had thrown it down the well. Curiously enough, they went on believing this even after the mislaid key was found under a sack of meal. The cows declared unanimously that Snowball crept into their stalls and milked them in their sleep. The rats, which had been troublesome that winter, were also said to be in league with Snowball.

Napoleon decreed that there should be a full investigation into Snowball's activities. With his dogs in attendance he set out and made a careful tour of inspection of the farm buildings, the other animals following at a respectful distance. At every few steps Napoleon stopped and snuffed the ground for traces of Snowball's footsteps, which, he said, he could detect by the smell. He snuffed in every corner, in the barn, in the cow-shed, in the hen-houses, in the vegetable garden, and found traces of Snowball almost everywhere. He would put his snout to the ground, give several deep sniffs, and exclaim in a terrible voice, "Snowball! He has been here! I can smell him distinctly!" and at the word "Snowball" all the dogs let out blood-curdling growls and showed their side teeth.

The animals were thoroughly frightened. It seemed to them as though Snowball were some kind of invisible influence, pervading the air about them and menacing them with all kinds of dangers. In the evening Squealer called them together, and with an alarmed expression on his face told them that he had some serious news to report.

"Comrades!" cried Squealer, making little nervous skips, "a most terrible thing has been discovered. Snowball has sold himself to Frederick of Pinchfield Farm, who is even now plotting to attack us and take our farm away from us! Snowball is to act as his guide when the attack begins. But there is worse than that. We had thought that Snowball's rebellion was caused simply by his vanity and ambition. But we were wrong, comrades. Do you know what the real reason was? Snowball was in league with Jones from the very start! He was Jones's secret agent all the time. It has all been proved by documents which he left behind him and which we have only just discovered. To my mind this explains a great deal, comrades. Did we not see for ourselves how he attempted—fortunately without success—to get us defeated and destroyed at the Battle of the Cowshed?"

The animals were stupefied. This was a wickedness far outdoing Snowball's destruction of the windmill. But it was some minutes before they could fully take it in. They all remembered, or thought they remembered, how they had seen Snowball charging ahead of them at the Battle of the Cowshed, how he had rallied and encouraged them at every turn, and how he had not paused for an instant even when the pellets from Jones's gun had wounded his back. At first it was a little difficult to see how this fitted in with his being on Jones's side: Even Boxer, who seldom asked questions, was puzzled. He lay down, tucked his fore hoofs beneath him, shut his eyes, and with a hard effort managed to formulate his thoughts.

"I do not believe that," he said. "Snowball fought bravely at the Battle of the Cowshed. I saw him myself. Did we not give him 'Animal Hero, first Class,' immediately afterwards?"

"That was our mistake, comrade. For we know now—it is all written down in the secret documents that we have found—that in reality he was trying to lure us to our doom."

"But he was wounded," said Boxer. "We all saw him running with blood."

"That was part of the arrangement!" cried Squealer. "Jones's shot only grazed him. I could show you this in his own writing, if you were able to read it. The plot was for Snowball, at the critical moment, to give the signal for flight and leave the field to the enemy. And he very nearly succeeded—I will even say, comrades, he *would* have succeeded if it had not been for our heroic Leader, Comrade Napoleon. Do you not remember how, just at the moment when Jones and his men had got inside the yard, Snowball suddenly turned and fled, and many animals followed him? And do you not remember, too, that it was just at that moment, when panic was spreading and all seemed lost, that Comrade Napoleon sprang forward with a cry of 'Death to Humanity!' and sank his teeth in Jones's leg? Surely you remember *that*, comrades?" exclaimed Squealer, frisking from side to side.

Now when Squealer described the scene so graphically, it seemed to the animals that they did remember it. At any rate, they remembered that at the critical moment of the battle Snowball had turned to flee. But Boxer was still a little uneasy.

"I do not believe that Snowball was a traitor at the beginning," he said finally. "What he has done since is different. But I believe that at the Battle of the Cowshed he was a good comrade."

"Our Leader, Comrade Napoleon," announced Squealer,

speaking very slowly and firmly, "has stated categorically—categorically, comrade—that Snowball was Jones's agent from the very beginning—yes, and from long before the Rebellion was ever thought of."

"Ah, that is different!" said Boxer. "If Comrade Napoleon says it, it must be right."

"That is the true spirit, comrade!" cried Squealer, but it was noticed he cast a very ugly look at Boxer with his little twinkling eyes. He turned to go, then paused and added impressively: "I warn every animal on this farm to keep his eyes very wide open. For we have reason to think that some of Snowball's secret agents are lurking among us at this moment! "

Four days later, in the late afternoon, Napoleon ordered all the animals to assemble in the yard. When they were all gathered together, Napoleon emerged from the farmhouse, wearing both his medals (for he had recently awarded himself "Animal Hero, First Class," and "Animal Hero, Second Class"), with his nine huge dogs frisking round him and uttering growls that sent shivers down all the animals' spines. They all cowered silently in their places, seeming to know in advance that some terrible thing was about to happen.

Napoleon stood sternly surveying his audience; then he uttered a high-pitched whimper. Immediately the dogs bounded forward, seized four of the pigs by the ear and dragged them, squealing with pain and terror, to Napoleon's feet. The pigs' ears were bleeding, the dogs had tasted blood, and for a few moments they appeared to go quite mad. To the amazement of everybody, three of them flung themselves upon Boxer. Boxer saw them coming and put out his great hoof, caught a dog in mid-air, and pinned him to the ground. The dog shrieked for mercy and the other two fled with their tails between their legs. Boxer looked at Napoleon to know whether he should crush the dog to death or let it go. Napoleon appeared to change countenance, and sharply ordered Boxer to let the dog go, whereat Boxer lifted his hoof, and the dog slunk away, bruised and howling.

Presently the tumult died down. The four pigs waited, trembling, with guilt written on every line of their countenances. Napoleon now called upon them to confess their crimes. They were the same four pigs as had protested when Napoleon abolished the Sunday Meetings. Without any further prompting they confessed that they had been secretly in touch with Snowball ever since his expulsion, that they had collaborated with him in destroying the windmill, and that they had entered into an agreement with him to hand over Animal Farm to Mr. Frederick. They added that Snowball had privately admitted to them that he had been Jones's secret agent for years past. When they had finished their confession, the dogs promptly tore their throats out, and in a terrible voice Napoleon demanded whether any other animal had anything to confess.

The three hens who had been the ringleaders in the attempted rebellion over the eggs now came forward and stated that Snowball had appeared to them in a dream and incited them to disobey Napoleon's orders. They, too, were slaughtered. Then a goose came forward and confessed to having secreted six ears of corn during the last year's harvest and eaten them in the night. Then a sheep confessed to having urinated in the drinking pool—urged to do this, so she said, by Snowball—and two other sheep confessed to having murdered an old ram, an especially devoted follower of Napoleon, by chasing him round and round a bonfire when he was suffering from a cough. They were all slain on the spot. And so the tale of confessions and executions went on, until there was a pile of corpses lying before Napoleon's feet and the air was heavy with the smell of blood, which had been unknown there since the expulsion of Jones.

When it was all over, the remaining animals, except for the pigs and dogs, crept away in a body. They were shaken and miserable. They did not know which was more shocking—the treachery of the animals who had leagued themselves with Snowball, or the cruel retribution they had just witnessed. In the old days there had often been scenes of bloodshed equally terrible, but it seemed to all of them that it was far worse now that it was happening among themselves. Since Jones had left the farm, until today, no animal had killed another animal. Not even a rat had been killed. They had made their way on to the little knoll where the half-finished windmill stood, and with one accord they all lay down as though huddling together for warmth—Clover, Muriel, Benjamin, the cows, the sheep, and a whole flock of geese and hens—everyone, indeed, except the cat, who had suddenly disappeared just before Napoleon ordered the animals to assemble. For some time nobody spoke. Only Boxer remained on his feet. He fidgeted to and fro, swishing his long black tail against his sides and occasionally uttering a little whinny of surprise. Finally he said:

"I do not understand it. I would not have believed that such things could happen on our farm. It must be due to some fault in ourselves. The solution, as I see it, is to work harder. From now onwards I shall get up a full hour earlier in the mornings."

And he moved off at his lumbering trot and made for the quarry. Having got there, he collected two successive loads of stone and dragged them down to the windmill before retiring for the night.

The animals huddled about Clover, not speaking. The knoll where they were lying gave them a wide prospect across the countryside. Most of Animal Farm was within their view—the long pasture stretching down to the main road, the hayfield, the spinney, the drinking pool, the ploughed fields where the young wheat was thick and green, and the red roofs of the farm buildings with the smoke curling from the chimneys. It was a clear spring evening. The grass and the bursting hedges were gilded by the level rays of the sun. Never had the farm—and with a kind of surprise they remembered that it was their own farm, every inch of it their own property—appeared to the animals so desirable a place. As Clover looked down the hillside her eyes filled with tears. If she could have spoken her thoughts, it would have been to say that this was not what they had aimed at when they had set themselves years ago to work for the overthrow of the human race. These scenes of terror and slaughter were not what they had looked forward to on that night when old Major first stirred them to rebellion. If she herself had had any picture of the future, it had been of a society of animals set free from hunger and the whip, all equal, each working according to his capacity, the strong protecting the weak, as she had protected the lost brood of ducklings with her foreleg on the night of Major's speech. Instead—she did not know why—they had come to a time when no one dared speak his mind, when fierce, growling dogs roamed everywhere, and when you had to watch your comrades torn to pieces after confessing to shocking crimes. There was no thought of rebellion or disobedience in her mind. She knew that, even as things were, they were far better off than they had been in the days of Jones, and that before all else it was needful to prevent the return of the human beings. Whatever happened she would remain faithful, work hard, carry out the orders that were given to her, and accept the leadership of Napoleon. But still, it was not for this that she and all the other animals had hoped and toiled. It was not for this that they had built the windmill and faced the bullets of Jones's gun. Such were her thoughts, though she lacked the words to express them.

At last, feeling this to be in some way a substitute for the words she was unable to find, she began to sing *Beasts of England*. The other animals sitting round her took it up, and they sang it three times over—very tunefully, but slowly and mournfully, in a way they had never sung it before.

They had just finished singing it for the third time when Squealer, attended by two dogs, approached them with the air of having something important to say. He announced that, by a special decree of Comrade Napoleon, *Beasts of England* had been abolished. From now onwards it was forbidden to sing it.

The animals were taken aback.

"Why?" cried Muriel.

"It's no longer needed, comrade," said Squealer stiffly.

"*Beasts of England* was the song of the Rebellion. But the Rebellion is now completed. The execution of the traitors this afternoon was the final act. The enemy both external and internal has been defeated. In *Beasts of England* we expressed our longing for a better society in days to come. But that society has now been established. Clearly this song has no longer any purpose."

Frightened though they were, some of the animals might possibly have protested, but at this moment the sheep set up their usual bleating of "Four legs good, two legs bad," which went on for several minutes and put an end to the discussion.

So *Beasts of England* was heard no more. In its place Minimus, the poet, had composed another song which began:

Animal Farm, Animal Farm,
Never through me shalt thou come to harm!

and this was sung every Sunday morning after the hoisting of the flag. But somehow neither the words nor the tune ever seemed to the animals to come up to *Beasts of England.*

Chapter VIII

A few days later, when the terror caused by the executions had died down, some of the animals remembered—or thought they remembered—that the Sixth Commandment decreed "No animal shall kill any other animal." And though no one cared to mention it in the hearing of the pigs or the dogs, it was felt that the killings which had taken place did not square with this. Clover asked Benjamin to read her the Sixth Commandment, and when Benjamin, as usual, said that he refused to meddle in such matters, she fetched Muriel. Muriel read the Commandment for her. It ran: "No animal shall kill any other animal *without cause*." Somehow or other, the last two words had slipped out of the animals' memory. But they saw now that the Commandment had not been violated; for clearly there was good reason for killing the traitors who had leagued themselves with Snowball.

Throughout the year the animals worked even harder than they had worked in the previous year To rebuild the windmill, with walls twice as thick as before, and to finish it by the appointed date, together with the regular work of the farm, was a tremendous labour. There were times when it seemed to the animals that they worked longer hours and fed no better than they had done in Jones's day. On Sunday mornings Squealer, holding down a long strip of paper with his trotter, would read out to them lists of figures proving that the production of every class of foodstuff had increased by two hundred per cent, three hundred per cent, or five hundred per cent, as the case might be. The animals saw no reason to disbelieve him, especially as they could no longer remember very clearly what conditions had been like before the Rebellion. All the same, there were days when they felt that they would sooner have had less figures and more food.

All orders were now issued through Squealer or one of the other pigs. Napoleon himself was not seen in public as often as once in a fortnight. When he did appear, he was attended not only by his retinue of dogs but by a black cockerel who marched in front of him and acted as a kind of trumpeter, letting out a loud "cock-a-doodle-doo" before Napoleon spoke. Even in the farmhouse, it was said, Napoleon inhabited separate apartments from the others. He took his meals alone, with two dogs to wait upon him, and always ate from the Crown Derby dinner service which had been in the glass cupboard in the drawing-room. It was also announced that the gun would be fired every year on Napoleon's birthday, as well as on the other two anniversaries.

Napoleon was now never spoken of simply as "Napoleon." He was always referred to in formal style as "our Leader, Comrade Napoleon," and the pigs liked to invent for him such titles as Father of All Animals, Terror of Mankind, Protector of the Sheep-fold, Ducklings' Friend, and the like. In his speeches, Squealer would talk with the tears rolling down his cheeks of Napoleon's wisdom, the goodness of his heart, and the deep love he bore to all animals everywhere, even and especially the unhappy animals who still lived in ignorance and slavery on other farms. It had become usual to give Napoleon the credit for every successful achievement and every stroke of good fortune. You would often hear one hen remark to another, "Under the guidance of our Leader, Comrade Napoleon, I have laid five eggs in six days"; or two cows, enjoying a drink at the pool, would exclaim, "Thanks to the leadership of Comrade Napoleon, how excellent this water tastes!" The general feeling on the farm was well expressed in a poem entitled *Comrade Napoleon,* which was composed by Minimus and which ran as follows·

Friend of fatherless!
Fountain of happiness!
Lord of the swill-bucket! Oh, how my soul is on
Fire when I gaze at thy
Calm and commanding eye,
Like the sun in the sky,
Comrade Napoleon!

Thou are the giver of
All that thy creatures love,
Full belly twice a day, clean straw to roll upon;
Every beast great or small
Sleeps at peace in his stall,
Thou watchest over all,
Comrade Napoleon!

Had I a sucking-pig,
Ere he had grown as big
Even as a pint bottle or as a rolling-pin,

He should have learned to be
Faithful and true to thee,
Yes, his first squeak should be
"Comrade Napoleon!"

Napoleon approved of this poem and caused it to be inscribed on the wall of the big barn, at the opposite end from the Seven Commandments. It was surmounted by a portrait of Napoleon, in profile, executed by Squealer in white paint.

Meanwhile, through the agency of Whymper, Napoleon was engaged in complicated negotiations with Frederick and Pilkington. The pile of timber was still unsold. Of the two, Frederick was the more anxious to get hold of it, but he would not offer a reasonable price. At the same time there were renewed rumours that Frederick and his men were plotting to attack Animal Farm and to destroy the windmill, the building of which had aroused furious jealousy in him. Snowball was known to be still skulking on Pinchfield Farm. In the middle of the summer the animals were alarmed to hear that three hens had come forward and confessed that, inspired by Snowball, they had entered into a plot to murder Napoleon. They were executed immediately, and fresh precautions for Napoleon's safety were taken. Four dogs guarded his bed at night, one at each corner, and a young pig named Pinkeye was given the task of tasting all his food before he ate it, lest it should be poisoned.

At about the same time it was given out that Napoleon had arranged to sell the pile of timber to Mr. Pilkington; he was also going to enter into a regular agreement for the exchange of certain products between Animal Farm and

Foxwood. The relations between Napoleon and Pilkington, though they were only conducted through Whymper, were now almost friendly. The animals distrusted Pilkington, as a human being, but greatly preferred him to Frederick, whom they both feared and hated. As the summer wore on, and the windmill neared completion, the rumours of an impending treacherous attack grew stronger and stronger. Frederick, it was said, intended to bring against them twenty men all armed with guns, and he had already bribed the magistrates and police, so that if he could once get hold of the title-deeds of Animal Farm they would ask no questions. Moreover, terrible stories were leaking out from Pinchfield about the cruelties that Frederick practised upon his animals. He had flogged an old horse to death, he starved his cows, he had killed a dog by throwing it into the furnace, he amused himself in the evenings by making cocks fight with splinters of razor-blade tied to their spurs. The animals' blood boiled with rage when they heard of these things being done to their comrades, and sometimes they clamoured to be allowed to go out in a body and attack Pinchfield Farm, drive out the humans, and set the animals free. But Squealer counselled them to avoid rash actions and trust in Comrade Napoleon's strategy.

Nevertheless, feeling against Frederick continued to run high. One Sunday morning Napoleon appeared in the barn and explained that he had never at any time contemplated selling the pile of timber to Frederick; he considered it beneath his dignity, he said, to have dealings with scoundrels of that description. The pigeons who were still sent out to spread tidings of the Rebellion were forbidden to set foot anywhere on Foxwood, and were also ordered to drop their former slogan of "Death to Humanity" in favour of "Death to Frederick." In the late summer yet another of Snowball's machinations was laid bare. The wheat crop was full of weeds, and it was discovered that on one of his nocturnal visits Snowball had mixed weed seeds with the seed corn. A gander who had been privy to the plot had confessed his guilt to Squealer and immediately committed suicide by swallowing deadly nightshade berries. The animals now also learned that Snowball had never—as many of them had believed hitherto—received the order of "Animal Hero, First Class." This was merely a legend which had been spread some time after the Battle of the Cowshed by Snowball himself. So far from being decorated, he had been censured for showing cowardice in the battle. Once again some of the animals heard this with a certain bewilderment, but Squealer was soon able to convince them that their memories had been at fault.

In the autumn, by a tremendous, exhausting effort—for the harvest had to be gathered at almost the same time—the windmill was finished. The machinery had still to be installed, and Whymper was negotiating the purchase of it, but the structure was completed. In the teeth of every difficulty, in spite of inexperience, of primitive implements, of bad luck and of Snowball's treachery, the work had been finished punctually to the very day! Tired out but proud, the animals walked round and round their masterpiece, which appeared even more beautiful in their eyes than when it had been built the first time. Moreover, the walls were twice as thick as before. Nothing short of explosives would lay them low this time!

And when they thought of how they had laboured, what discouragements they had overcome, and the enormous difference that would be made in their lives when the sails were turning and the dynamos running—when they thought of all this, their tiredness forsook them and they gambolled round and round the windmill, uttering cries of triumph. Napoleon himself, attended by his dogs and his cockerel, came down to inspect the completed work; he personally congratulated the animals on their achievement, and announced that the mill would be named Napoleon Mill.

Two days later the animals were called together for a special meeting in the barn. They were struck dumb with surprise when Napoleon announced that he had sold the pile of timber to Frederick. Tomorrow Frederick's wagons would arrive and begin carting it away. Throughout the whole period of his seeming friendship with Pilkington, Napoleon had really been in secret agreement with Frederick.

All relations with Foxwood had been broken off; insulting messages had been sent to Pilkington. The pigeons had been told to avoid Pinchfield Farm and to alter their slogan from "Death to Frederick" to "Death to Pilkington." At the same time Napoleon assured the animals that the stories of an impending attack on Animal Farm were completely untrue, and that the tales about Frederick's cruelty to his own animals had been greatly exaggerated. All these rumours had probably originated with Snowball and his agents. It now appeared that Snowball was not, after all, hiding on Pinchfield Farm, and in fact had never been there in his life: he was living—in considerable luxury, so it was said—at Foxwood, and had in reality been a pensioner of Pilkington for years past.

The pigs were in ecstasies over Napoleon's cunning. By seeming to be friendly with Pilkington he had forced Frederick to raise his price by twelve pounds. But the superior quality of Napoleon's mind, said Squealer, was shown in the fact that he trusted nobody, not even Frederick. Frederick had wanted to pay for the timber with something called a cheque, which, it seemed, was a piece of paper with a promise to pay written upon it. But Napoleon was too clever for him. He had demanded payment in real five-pound notes, which were to be handed over before the timber was removed. Already Frederick had paid up; and the sum he had paid was just enough to buy the machinery for the windmill.

Meanwhile the timber was being carted away at high speed. When it was all gone, another special meeting was held in the barn for the animals to inspect Frederick's banknotes. Smiling beatifically, and wearing both his decorations, Napoleon reposed on a bed of straw on the platform, with the money at his side, neatly piled on a china dish from the farmhouse kitchen. The animals filed slowly past, and each gazed his fill. And Boxer put out his nose to sniff at the banknotes, and the flimsy white things stirred and rustled in his breath.

Three days later there was a terrible hullabaloo. Whymper, his face deadly pale, came racing up the path on his bicycle, flung it down in the yard and rushed straight into the farmhouse. The next moment a choking roar of rage sounded from Napoleon's apartments. The news of what had happened sped round the farm like wildfire. The banknotes were forgeries! Frederick had got the timber for nothing!

Napoleon called the animals together immediately and in a terrible voice pronounced the death sentence upon Frederick. When captured, he said, Frederick should be boiled alive. At the same time he warned them that after this treacherous deed the worst was to be expected. Frederick and his men might make their long-expected attack at any moment. Sentinels were placed at all the approaches to the farm. In addition, four pigeons were sent to Foxwood with a conciliatory message, which it was hoped might re-establish good relations with Pilkington.

The very next morning the attack came. The animals were at breakfast when the look-outs came racing in with the news that Frederick and his followers had already come through the five-barred gate. Boldly enough the animals sallied forth to meet them, but this time they did not have the easy victory that they had had in the Battle of the Cowshed. There were fifteen men, with half a dozen guns between them, and they opened fire as soon as they got within fifty yards. The animals could not face the terrible explosions and the stinging pellets, and in spite of the efforts of Napoleon and Boxer to rally them, they were soon driven back. A number of them were already wounded. They took refuge in the farm buildings and peeped cautiously out from chinks and knot-holes. The whole of the big pasture, including the windmill, was in the hands of the enemy. For the moment even Napoleon seemed at a loss. He paced up and down without a word, his tail rigid and twitching. Wistful glances were sent in the direction of Foxwood. If Pilkington and his men would help them, the day might yet be won. But at this moment the four pigeons, who had been sent out on the day before, returned, one of them bearing a scrap of paper from Pilkington. On it was pencilled the words: "Serves you right."

Meanwhile Frederick and his men had halted about the windmill. The animals watched them, and a murmur of dismay went round. Two of the men had produced a crowbar and a sledge hammer. They were going to knock the windmill down.

"Impossible!" cried Napoleon. "We have built the walls far too thick for that. They could not knock it down in a week. Courage, comrades!"

But Benjamin was watching the movements of the men intently. The two with the hammer and the crowbar were drilling a hole near the base of the windmill. Slowly, and with an air almost of amusement, Benjamin nodded his long muzzle.

"I thought so," he said. "Do you not see what they are doing? In another moment they are going to pack blasting powder into that hole."

Terrified, the animals waited. It was impossible now to venture out of the shelter of the buildings. After a few minutes the men were seen to be running in all directions. Then there was a deafening roar. The pigeons swirled into the air, and all the animals, except Napoleon, flung themselves flat on their bellies and hid their faces. When they got up again, a huge cloud of black smoke was hanging where the windmill had been. Slowly the breeze drifted it away. The windmill had ceased to exist!

At this sight the animals' courage returned to them. The fear and despair they had felt a moment earlier were drowned in their rage against this vile, contemptible act. A mighty cry for vengeance went up, and without waiting for further orders they charged forth in a body and made straight for the enemy. This time they did not heed the cruel pellets that swept over them like hail. It was a savage, bitter battle. The men fired again and again, and, when the animals got to close quarters, lashed out with their sticks and their heavy boots. A cow, three sheep, and two geese were killed, and nearly everyone was wounded. Even Napoleon, who was directing operations from the rear, had the tip of his tail chipped by a pellet. But the men did not go unscathed either. Three of them had their heads broken by blows from Boxer's hoofs; another was gored in the belly by a cow's horn; another had his trousers nearly torn off by Jessie and Bluebell. And when the nine dogs of Napoleon's own bodyguard, whom he had instructed to make a detour under cover of the hedge, suddenly appeared on the men's flank, baying ferociously, panic overtook them. They saw that they were in danger of being surrounded. Frederick shouted to his men to get out while the going was good, and the next moment the cowardly enemy was running for dear life. The animals chased them right down to the bottom of the field, and got in some last kicks at them as they forced their way through the thorn hedge.

They had won, but they were weary and bleeding. Slowly they began to limp back towards the farm. The sight of their dead comrades stretched upon the grass moved some of them to tears. And for a little while they halted in sorrowful silence at the place where the windmill had once stood. Yes, it was gone; almost the last trace of their labour was gone! Even the foundations were partially destroyed. And in rebuilding it they could not this time, as before, make use of the fallen stones. This time the stones had vanished too. The force of the explosion had flung them to distances of hundreds of yards. It was as though the windmill had never been.

As they approached the farm Squealer, who had unaccountably been absent during the fighting, came skipping towards them, whisking his tail and beaming with satisfaction. And the animals heard, from the direction of the farm buildings, the solemn booming of a gun.

"What is that gun firing for?" said Boxer.

"To celebrate our victory!" cried Squealer.

"What victory?" said Boxer. His knees were bleeding, he had lost a shoe and split his hoof, and a dozen pellets had lodged themselves in his hind leg.

"What victory, comrade? Have we not driven the enemy off our soil—the sacred soil of Animal Farm?"

"But they have destroyed the windmill. And we had worked on it for two years!"

"What matter? We will build another windmill. We will build six windmills if we feel like it. You do not appreciate, comrade, the mighty thing that we have done. The enemy was in occupation of this very ground that we stand upon. And now—thanks to the leadership of Comrade Napoleon—we have won every inch of it back again!"

"Then we have won back what we had before," said Boxer.

"That is our victory," said Squealer.

They limped into the yard. The pellets under the skin of Boxer's leg smarted painfully. He saw ahead of him the heavy labour of rebuilding the windmill from the foundations, and already in imagination he braced himself for the task. But for the first time it occurred to him that he was eleven years old and that perhaps his great muscles were not quite what they had once been.

But when the animals saw the green flag flying, and heard the gun firing again—seven times it was fired in all—and heard the speech that Napoleon made, congratulating them on their conduct, it did seem to them after all that they had won a great victory. The animals slain in the battle were given a solemn funeral. Boxer and Clover pulled the wagon which served as a hearse, and Napoleon himself walked at the head of the procession. Two whole days were given over to celebrations. There were songs, speeches, and more firing of the gun, and a special gift of an apple was bestowed on every animal, with two ounces of corn for each bird and three biscuits for each dog. It was announced that the battle would be called the Battle of the Windmill, and that Napoleon had created a new decoration, the Order of the Green Banner, which he had conferred upon himself. In the general rejoicings the unfortunate affair of the banknotes was forgotten.

It was a few days later than this that the pigs came upon a case of whisky in the cellars of the farmhouse. It had been overlooked at the time when the house was first occupied. That night there came from the farmhouse the sound of loud singing, in which, to everyone's surprise, the strains of *Beasts of England* were mixed up. At about half past nine Napoleon, wearing an old bowler hat of Mr. Jones's, was distinctly seen to emerge from the back door, gallop rapidly round the yard, and disappear indoors again. But in the morning a deep silence hung over the farmhouse. Not a pig appeared to be stirring. It was nearly nine o'clock when Squealer made his appearance, walking slowly and dejectedly, his eyes dull, his tail hanging limply behind him, and with every appearance of being seriously ill. He called the animals together and told them that he had a terrible piece of news to impart. Comrade Napoleon was dying!

A cry of lamentation went up. Straw was laid down outside the doors of the farmhouse, and the animals walked on tiptoe. With tears in their eyes they asked one another what they should do if their Leader were taken away from them. A rumour went round that Snowball had after all contrived to introduce poison into Napoleon's food. At eleven o'clock Squealer came out to make another announcement. As his last act upon earth, Comrade Napoleon had pronounced a solemn decree: the drinking of alcohol was to be punished by death.

By the evening, however, Napoleon appeared to be somewhat better, and the following morning Squealer was able to tell them that he was well on the way to recovery. By the evening of that day Napoleon was back at work, and on the next day it was learned that he had instructed Whymper to purchase in Willingdon some booklets on brewing and distilling. A week later Napoleon gave orders that the small paddock beyond the orchard, which it had previously been intended to set aside as a grazing-ground for animals who were past work, was to be ploughed up. It was given out that the pasture was exhausted and needed re-seeding; but it soon became known that Napoleon intended to sow it with barley.

About this time there occurred a strange incident which hardly anyone was able to understand. One night at about twelve o'clock there was a loud crash in the yard, and the animals rushed out of their stalls. It was a moonlit night. At the foot of the end wall of the big barn, where the Seven Commandments were written, there lay a ladder broken in two pieces. Squealer, temporarily stunned, was sprawling beside it, and near at hand there lay a lantern, a paint-brush, and an overturned pot of white paint. The dogs immediately made a ring round Squealer, and escorted him back to the farmhouse as soon as he was able to walk. None of the animals could form any idea as to what this meant, except old Benjamin, who nodded his muzzle with a knowing air, and seemed to understand, but would say nothing.

But a few days later Muriel, reading over the Seven Commandments to herself, noticed that there was yet another of them which the animals had remembered wrong. They had thought the Fifth Commandment was "No animal shall drink alcohol," but there were two words that they had forgotten. Actually the Commandment read: "No animal shall drink alcohol to *excess.*"

Chapter IX

Boxer's split hoof was a long time in healing. They had started the rebuilding of the windmill the day after the victory celebrations were ended. Boxer refused to take even a day off work, and made it a point of honour not to let it be seen that he was in pain. In the evenings he would admit privately to Clover that the hoof troubled him a great deal. Clover treated the hoof with poultices of herbs which she prepared by chewing them, and both she and Benjamin urged Boxer to work less hard. "A horse's lungs do not last for ever," she said to him. But Boxer would not listen. He had, he said, only one real ambition left—to see the windmill well under way before he reached the age for retirement.

At the beginning, when the laws of Animal Farm were first formulated, the retiring age had been fixed for horses and pigs at twelve, for cows at fourteen, for dogs at nine, for sheep at seven, and for hens and geese at five. Liberal old-age pensions had been agreed upon. As yet no animal had actually retired on pension, but of late the subject had been discussed more and more. Now that the small field beyond the orchard had been set aside for barley, it was rumoured that a corner of the large pasture was to be fenced off and turned into a grazing-ground for superannuated animals. For a horse, it was said, the pension would be five pounds of corn a day and, in winter, fifteen pounds of hay, with a carrot or possibly an apple on public holidays. Boxer's twelfth birthday was due in the late summer of the following year.

Meanwhile life was hard. The winter was as cold as the last one had been, and food was even shorter. Once again all rations were reduced, except those of the pigs and the dogs. A too rigid equality in rations, Squealer explained, would have been contrary to the principles of Animalism. In any case he had no difficulty in proving to the other animals that they were not in reality short of food, whatever the appearances might be. For the time being, certainly, it had been found necessary to make a readjustment of rations (Squealer always spoke of it as a "readjustment," never as a "reduction"), but in comparison with the days of Jones, the improvement was enormous. Reading out the figures in a shrill, rapid voice, he proved to them in detail that they had more oats, more hay, more turnips than they had had in Jones's day, that they worked shorter hours, that their drinking water was of better quality, that they lived longer, that a larger proportion of their young ones survived infancy, and that they had more straw in their stalls and suffered less from fleas. The animals believed every word of it. Truth to tell, Jones and all he stood for had almost faded out of their memories. They knew that life nowadays was harsh and bare, that they were often hungry and often cold, and that they were usually working when they were not asleep. But doubtless it had been worse in the old days. They were glad to believe so. Besides, in those days they had been slaves and now they were free, and that made all the difference, as Squealer did not fail to point out.

There were many more mouths to feed now. In the autumn the four sows had all littered about simultaneously, producing thirty-one young pigs between them. The young pigs were piebald, and as Napoleon was the only boar on the farm, it was possible to guess at their parentage. It was announced that later, when bricks and timber had been purchased, a schoolroom would be built in the farmhouse garden. For the time being, the young pigs were given their instruction by Napoleon himself in the farmhouse kitchen. They took their exercise in the garden, and were discouraged from playing with the other young animals. About this time, too, it was laid down as a rule that when a pig and any other animal met on the path, the other animal must stand aside: and also that all pigs, of whatever degree, were to have the privilege of wearing green ribbons on their tails on Sundays.

The farm had had a fairly successful year, but was still short of money. There were the bricks, sand, and lime for the schoolroom to be purchased, and it would also be necessary to begin saving up again for the machinery for the windmill. Then there were lamp oil and candles for the house, sugar for Napoleon's own table (he forbade this to the other pigs, on the ground that it made them fat), and all the usual replacements such as tools, nails, string, coal, wire, scrap-iron, and dog biscuits. A stump of hay and part of the potato crop were sold off, and the contract for eggs was increased to six hundred a week, so that that year the hens barely hatched enough chicks to keep their numbers at the same level. Rations, reduced in December, were reduced again in February, and lanterns in the stalls were forbidden to save oil. But the pigs seemed comfortable enough, and in fact were putting on weight if anything. One afternoon in late February a warm, rich, appetising scent, such as the animals had never smelt before, wafted itself across the yard from the little brew-house, which had been disused in Jones's time, and which stood beyond the kitchen. Someone said it was the smell of cooking barley. The animals sniffed the air hungrily and wondered whether a warm mash was being prepared for their supper. But no warm mash appeared, and on the following Sunday it was announced that from now onwards all barley would be reserved for the pigs. The field beyond the orchard had already been sown with barley. And the news soon leaked out that every pig was now receiving a ration of a pint of beer daily, with half a gallon for Napoleon himself, which was always served to him in the Crown Derby soup tureen.

But if there were hardships to be borne, they were partly offset by the fact that life nowadays had a greater dignity than it had had before. There were more songs, more speeches, more processions. Napoleon had commanded that once a week there should be held something called a Spontaneous Demonstration, the object of which was to celebrate the struggles and triumphs of Animal Farm. At the appointed time the animals would leave their work and march round the precincts of the farm in military formation, with the pigs leading, then the horses, then the cows, then the sheep, and then the poultry. The dogs flanked the procession and at the head of all marched Napoleon's black cockerel. Boxer and Clover always carried between them a green banner marked with the hoof and the horn and the caption, "Long live Comrade Napoleon! " Afterwards there were recitations of poems composed in Napoleon's honour, and a speech by

Squealer giving particulars of the latest increases in the production of foodstuffs, and on occasion a shot was fired from the gun. The sheep were the greatest devotees of the Spontaneous Demonstration, and if anyone complained (as a few animals sometimes did, when no pigs or dogs were near) that they wasted time and meant a lot of standing about in the cold, the sheep were sure to silence him with a tremendous bleating of "Four legs good, two legs bad!" But by and large the animals enjoyed these celebrations. They found it comforting to be reminded that, after all, they were truly their own masters and that the work they did was for their own benefit. So that, what with the songs, the processions, Squealer's lists of figures, the thunder of the gun, the crowing of the cockerel, and the fluttering of the flag, they were able to forget that their bellies were empty, at least part of the time.

In April, Animal Farm was proclaimed a Republic, and it became necessary to elect a President. There was only one candidate, Napoleon, who was elected unanimously. On the same day it was given out that fresh documents had been discovered which revealed further details about Snowball's complicity with Jones. It now appeared that Snowball had not, as the animals had previously imagined, merely attempted to lose the Battle of the Cowshed by means of a stratagem, but had been openly fighting on Jones's side. In fact, it was he who had actually been the leader of the human forces, and had charged into battle with the words "Long live Humanity!" on his lips. The wounds on Snowball's back, which a few of the animals still remembered to have seen, had been inflicted by Napoleon's teeth.

In the middle of the summer Moses the raven suddenly reappeared on the farm, after an absence of several years He was quite unchanged, still did no work, and talked in the same strain as ever about Sugarcandy Mountain. He would perch on a stump, flap his black wings, and talk by the hour to anyone who would listen. "Up there, comrades," he would say solemnly, pointing to the sky with his large beak—"up there, just on the other side of that dark cloud that you can see—there it lies, Sugarcandy Mountain, that happy country where we poor animals shall rest for ever from our labours!" He even claimed to have been there on one of his higher flights, and to have seen the everlasting fields of clover and the linseed cake and lump sugar growing on the hedges. Many of the animals believed him. Their lives now, they reasoned, were hungry and laborious; was it not right and just that a better world should exist somewhere else? A thing that was difficult to determine was the attitude of the pigs towards Moses. They all declared contemptuously that his stories about Sugarcandy Mountain were lies, and yet they allowed him to remain on the farm, not working, with an allowance of a gill of beer a day.

After his hoof had healed up, Boxer worked harder than ever. Indeed, all the animals worked like slaves that year. Apart from the regular work of the farm, and the rebuilding of the windmill, there was the schoolhouse for the young pigs, which was started in March. Sometimes the long hours on insufficient food were hard to bear, but Boxer never faltered. In nothing that he said or did was there any sign that his strength was not what it had been. It was only his appearance that was a little altered; his hide was less shiny than it had used to be, and his great haunches seemed to have shrunken. The others said, "Boxer will pick up when the spring grass comes on"; but the spring came and Boxer grew no fatter. Sometimes on the slope leading to the top of the quarry, when he braced his muscles against the weight of some vast boulder, it seemed that nothing kept him on his feet except the will to continue. At such times his lips were seen to form the words, "I will work harder"; he had no voice left. Once again Clover and Benjamin warned him to take care of his health, but Boxer paid no attention. His twelfth birthday was approaching. He did not care what happened so long as a good store of stone was accumulated before he went on pension.

Late one evening in the summer, a sudden rumour ran round the farm that something had happened to Boxer. He had gone out alone to drag a load of stone down to the windmill. And sure enough, the rumour was true. A few minutes later two pigeons came racing in with the news: "Boxer has fallen! He is lying on his side and can't get up!"

About half the animals on the farm rushed out to the knoll where the windmill stood. There lay Boxer, between the shafts of the cart, his neck stretched out, unable even to raise his head. His eyes were glazed, his sides matted with sweat. A thin stream of blood had trickled out of his mouth. Clover dropped to her knees at his side.

"Boxer!" she cried, "how are you?"

"It is my lung," said Boxer in a weak voice. "It does not matter. I think you will be able to finish the windmill without me. There is a pretty good store of stone accumulated. I had only another month to go in any case. To tell you the truth, I had been looking forward to my retirement. And perhaps, as Benjamin is growing old too, they will let him retire at the same time and be a companion to me."

"We must get help at once," said Clover. "Run, somebody, and tell Squealer what has happened."

All the other animals immediately raced back to the farmhouse to give Squealer the news. Only Clover remained, and Benjamin, who lay down at Boxer's side, and, without speaking, kept the flies off him with his long tail.

After about a quarter of an hour Squealer appeared, full of sympathy and concern. He said that Comrade Napoleon had learned with the very deepest distress of this misfortune to one of the most loyal workers on the farm, and was already making arrangements to send Boxer to be treated in the hospital at Willingdon. The animals felt a little uneasy at this. Except for Mollie and Snowball, no other animal had ever left the farm, and they did not like to think of their sick comrade in the hands of human beings. However, Squealer easily convinced them that the veterinary surgeon in Willingdon could treat Boxer's case more satisfactorily than could be done on the farm. And about half an hour later, when Boxer had somewhat recovered, he was with difficulty got on to his feet, and managed to limp back to his stall, where Clover and Benjamin had prepared a good bed of straw for him.

For the next two days Boxer remained in his stall. The pigs had sent out a large bottle of pink medicine which they had found in the medicine chest in the bathroom, and Clover administered it to Boxer twice a day after meals. In the evenings she lay in his stall and talked to him, while Benjamin kept the flies off him. Boxer professed not to be sorry for what had happened. If he made a good recovery, he might expect to live another three years, and he looked forward to the peaceful days that he would spend in the corner of the big pasture. It would be the first time that he had had leisure to study and improve his mind. He intended, he said, to devote the rest of his life to learning the remaining twenty-two letters of the alphabet.

However, Benjamin and Clover could only be with Boxer after working hours, and it was in the middle of the day when the van came to take him away. The animals were all at work weeding turnips under the supervision of a pig, when they were astonished to see Benjamin come galloping from the direction of the farm buildings, braying at the top of his voice. It was the first time that they had ever seen Benjamin excited—indeed, it was the first time that anyone had ever seen him gallop. "Quick, quick!" he shouted. "Come at once! They're taking Boxer away!" Without waiting for orders from the pig, the animals broke off work and raced back to the farm buildings. Sure enough, there in the yard was a large closed van, drawn by two horses, with lettering on its side and a sly-looking man in a low-crowned bowler hat sitting on the driver's seat. And Boxer's stall was empty.

The animals crowded round the van. "Good-bye, Boxer!" they chorused, "good-bye!"

"Fools! Fools!" shouted Benjamin, prancing round them and stamping the earth with his small hoofs. "Fools! Do you not see what is written on the side of that van?"

That gave the animals pause, and there was a hush. Muriel began to spell out the words. But Benjamin pushed her aside and in the midst of a deadly silence he read:

"'Alfred Simmonds, Horse Slaughterer and Glue Boiler, Willingdon. Dealer in Hides and Bone-Meal. Kennels Supplied.' Do you not understand what that means? They are taking Boxer to the knacker's!"

A cry of horror burst from all the animals. At this moment the man on the box whipped up his horses and the van moved out of the yard at a smart trot. All the animals followed, crying out at the tops of their voices. Clover forced her way to the front. The van began to gather speed. Clover tried to stir her stout limbs to a gallop, and achieved a canter. "Boxer!" she cried. "Boxer! Boxer! Boxer!" And just at this moment, as though he had heard the uproar outside, Boxer's face, with the white stripe down his nose, appeared at the small window at the back of the van.

"Boxer!" cried Clover in a terrible voice. "Boxer! Get out! Get out quickly! They're taking you to your death!"

All the animals took up the cry of "Get out, Boxer, get out!" But the van was already gathering speed and drawing away from them. It was uncertain whether Boxer had understood what Clover had said. But a moment later his face disappeared from the window and there was the sound of a tremendous drumming of hoofs inside the van. He was trying to kick his way out. The time had been when a few kicks from Boxer's hoofs would have smashed the van to matchwood. But alas! his strength had left him; and in a few moments the sound of drumming hoofs grew fainter and died away. In desperation the animals began appealing to the two horses which drew the van to stop. "Comrades, comrades!" they shouted. "Don't take your own brother to his death! "

But the stupid brutes, too ignorant to realise what was happening, merely set back their ears and quickened their pace. Boxer's face did not reappear at the window. Too late, someone thought of racing ahead and shutting the five-barred gate; but in another moment the van was through it and rapidly disappearing down the road. Boxer was never seen again.

Three days later it was announced that he had died in the hospital at Willingdon, in spite of receiving every attention a horse could have. Squealer came to announce the news to the others. He had, he said, been present during Boxer's last hours.

"It was the most affecting sight I have ever seen!" said Squealer, lifting his trotter and wiping away a tear. "I was at his bedside at the very last. And at the end, almost too weak to speak, he whispered in my ear that his sole sorrow was to have passed on before the windmill was finished. 'Forward, comrades!' he whispered. 'Forward in the name of the Rebellion. Long live Animal Farm! Long live Comrade Napoleon! Napoleon is always right.' Those were his very last words, comrades."

Here Squealer's demeanour suddenly changed. He fell silent for a moment, and his little eyes darted suspicious glances from side to side before he proceeded.

It had come to his knowledge, he said, that a foolish and wicked rumour had been circulated at the time of Boxer's removal. Some of the animals had noticed that the van which took Boxer away was marked "Horse Slaughterer," and had actually jumped to the conclusion that Boxer was being sent to the knacker's. It was almost unbelievable, said Squealer, that any animal could be so stupid. Surely, he cried indignantly, whisking his tail and skipping from side to side, surely they knew their beloved Leader, Comrade Napoleon, better than that? But the explanation was really very simple. The van had previously been the property of the knacker, and had been bought by the veterinary surgeon, who had not yet painted the old name out. That was how the mistake had arisen.

The animals were enormously relieved to hear this. And when Squealer went on to give further graphic details of Boxer's death-bed, the admirable care he had received, and the expensive medicines for which Napoleon had paid without a thought as to the cost, their last doubts disappeared and the sorrow that they felt for their comrade's death was tempered by the thought that at least he had died happy.

Napoleon himself appeared at the meeting on the following Sunday morning and pronounced a short oration in Boxer's honour. It had not been possible, he said, to bring back their lamented comrade's remains for interment on the farm, but he had ordered a large wreath to be made from the laurels in the farmhouse garden and sent down to be placed on Boxer's grave. And in a few days' time the pigs intended to hold a memorial banquet in Boxer's honour. Napoleon ended his speech with a reminder of Boxer's two favourite maxims, "I will work harder" and "Comrade Napoleon is always right"—maxims, he said, which every animal would do well to adopt as his own.

On the day appointed for the banquet, a grocer's van drove up from Willingdon and delivered a large wooden crate at the farmhouse. That night there was the sound of uproarious singing, which was followed by what sounded like a violent quarrel and ended at about eleven o'clock with a tremendous crash of glass. No one stirred in the farmhouse before noon on the following day, and the word went round that from somewhere or other the pigs had acquired the money to buy themselves another case of whisky.

Chapter X

Years passed. The seasons came and went, the short animal lives fled by. A time came when there was no one who remembered the old days before the Rebellion, except Clover, Benjamin, Moses the raven, and a number of the pigs.

Muriel was dead; Bluebell, Jessie, and Pincher were dead. Jones too was dead—he had died in an inebriates' home in another part of the country. Snowball was forgotten. Boxer was forgotten, except by the few who had known him. Clover was an old stout mare now, stiff in the joints and with a tendency to rheumy eyes. She was two years past the retiring age, but in fact no animal had ever actually retired. The talk of setting aside a corner of the pasture for superannuated animals had long since been dropped. Napoleon was now a mature boar of twenty-four stone. Squealer was so fat that he could with difficulty see out of his eyes. Only old Benjamin was much the same as ever, except for being a little greyer about the muzzle, and, since Boxer's death, more morose and taciturn than ever.

There were many more creatures on the farm now, though the increase was not so great as had been expected in earlier years. Many animals had been born to whom the Rebellion was only a dim tradition, passed on by word of mouth, and others had been bought who had never heard mention of such a thing before their arrival. The farm possessed three horses now besides Clover. They were fine upstanding beasts, willing workers and good comrades, but very stupid. None of them proved able to learn the alphabet beyond the letter B. They accepted everything that they were told about the Rebellion and the principles of Animalism, especially from Clover, for whom they had an almost filial respect; but it was doubtful whether they understood very much of it.

The farm was more prosperous now, and better organised: it had even been enlarged by two fields which had been bought from Mr. Pilkington. The windmill had been successfully completed at last, and the farm possessed a threshing machine and a hay elevator of its own, and various new buildings had been added to it. Whymper had bought himself a dogcart. The windmill, however, had not after all been used for generating electrical power. It was used for milling corn, and brought in a handsome money profit. The animals were hard at work building yet another windmill; when that one was finished, so it was said, the dynamos would be installed. But the luxuries of which Snowball had once taught the animals to dream, the stalls with electric light and hot and cold water, and the three-day week, were no longer talked about. Napoleon had denounced such ideas as contrary to the spirit of Animalism. The truest happiness, he said, lay in working hard and living frugally.

Somehow it seemed as though the farm had grown richer without making the animals themselves any richer—except, of course, for the pigs and the dogs. Perhaps this was partly because there were so many pigs and so many dogs. It was not that these creatures did not work, after their fashion. There was, as Squealer was never tired of explaining, endless work in the supervision and organisation of the farm. Much of this work was of a kind that the other animals were too ignorant to understand. For example, Squealer told them that the pigs had to expend enormous labours every day upon mysterious things called "files," "reports," "minutes," and "memoranda." These were large sheets of paper which had to be closely covered with writing, and as soon as they were so covered, they were burnt in the furnace. This was of the highest importance for the welfare of the farm, Squealer said. But still, neither pigs nor dogs produced any food by their own labour; and there were very many of them, and their appetites were always good.

As for the others, their life, so far as they knew, was as it had always been. They were generally hungry, they slept on straw, they drank from the pool, they laboured in the fields; in winter they were troubled by the cold, and in summer by the flies. Sometimes the older ones among them racked their dim memories and tried to determine whether in the early days of the Rebellion, when Jones's expulsion was still recent, things had been better or worse than now. They could not remember. There was nothing with which they could compare their present lives: they had nothing to go upon except Squealer's lists of figures, which invariably demonstrated that everything was getting better and better. The animals found the problem insoluble; in any case, they had little time for speculating on such things now. Only old Benjamin professed to remember every detail of his long life and to know that things never had been, nor ever could be much better or much worse—hunger, hardship, and disappointment being, so he said, the unalterable law of life.

And yet the animals never gave up hope. More, they never lost, even for an instant, their sense of honour and privilege in being members of Animal Farm. They were still the only farm in the whole country—in all England!—owned and operated by animals. Not one of them, not even the youngest, not even the newcomers who had been brought from farms ten or twenty miles away, ever ceased to marvel at that. And when they heard the gun booming and saw the green flag fluttering at the masthead, their hearts swelled with imperishable pride, and the talk turned always towards the old heroic days, the expulsion of Jones, the writing of the Seven Commandments, the great battles in which the human invaders had been defeated. None of the old dreams had been abandoned. The Republic of the Animals which Major had. foretold, when the green fields of England should be untrodden by human feet, was still believed in. Some day it was coming: it might not be soon, it might not be with in the lifetime of any animal now living, but still it was coming. Even the tune of *Beasts of England* was perhaps hummed secretly here and there: at any rate, it was a fact that every animal on the farm knew it, though no one would have dared to sing it aloud. It might be that their lives were hard and that not all of their hopes had been fulfilled; but they were conscious that they were not as other animals. If they were hungry, it was not from feeding tyrannical human beings; if they worked hard, at least they worked for themselves. No creature among them went upon two legs. No creature called any other creature "Master." All animals were equal.

One day in early summer Squealer ordered the sheep to

follow him, and led them out to a piece of waste ground at the other end of the farm, which had become overgrown with birch saplings. The sheep spent the whole day there browsing at the leaves under Squealer's supervision. In the evening he returned to the farmhouse himself, but, as it was warm weather, told the sheep to stay where they were. It ended by their remaining there for a whole week, during which time the other animals saw nothing of them. Squealer was with them for the greater part of every day. He was, he said, teaching them to sing a new song, for which privacy was needed.

It was just after the sheep had returned, on a pleasant evening when the animals had finished work and were making their way back to the farm buildings, that the terrified neighing of a horse sounded from the yard. Startled, the animals stopped in their tracks. It was Clover's voice. She neighed again, and all the animals broke into a gallop and rushed into the yard. Then they saw what Clover had seen.

It was a pig walking on his hind legs.

Yes, it was Squealer. A little awkwardly, as though not quite used to supporting his considerable bulk in that position, but with perfect balance, he was strolling across the yard. And a moment later, out from the door of the farmhouse came a long file of pigs, all walking on their hind legs. Some did it better than others, one or two were even a trifle unsteady and looked as though they would have liked the support of a stick, but every one of them made his way right round the yard successfully. And finally there was a tremendous baying of dogs and a shrill crowing from the black cockerel, and out came Napoleon himself, majestically upright, casting haughty glances from side to side, and with his dogs gambolling round him.

He carried a whip in his trotter.

There was a deadly silence. Amazed, terrified, huddling together, the animals watched the long line of pigs march slowly round the yard. It was as though the world had turned upside-down. Then there came a moment when the first shock had worn off and when, in spite of everything—in spite of their terror of the dogs, and of the habit, developed through long years, of never complaining, never criticising, no matter what happened—they might have uttered some word of protest. But just at that moment, as though at a signal, all the sheep burst out into a tremendous bleating of—

"Four legs good, two legs *better*! Four legs good, two legs *better*! Four legs good, two legs *better!*"

It went on for five minutes without stopping. And by the time the sheep had quieted down, the chance to utter any protest had passed, for the pigs had marched back into the farmhouse.

Benjamin felt a nose nuzzling at his shoulder. He looked round. It was Clover. Her old eyes looked dimmer than ever. Without saying anything, she tugged gently at his mane and led him round to the end of the big barn, where the Seven Commandments were written. For a minute or two they stood gazing at the tatted wall with its white lettering.

"My sight is failing," she said finally. "Even when I was young I could not have read what was written there. But it appears to me that that wall looks different. Are the Seven Commandments the same as they used to be, Benjamin?"

For once Benjamin consented to break his rule, and he read out to her what was written on the wall. There was nothing there now except a single Commandment. It ran:

ALL ANIMALS ARE EQUAL
BUT SOME ANIMALS ARE MORE EQUAL THAN OTHERS

After that it did not seem strange when next day the pigs who were supervising the work of the farm all carried whips in their trotters. It did not seem strange to learn that the pigs had bought themselves a wireless set, were arranging to install a telephone, and had taken out subscriptions to John *Bull*, *TitBits*, and the *Daily Mirror*. It did not seem strange when Napoleon was seen strolling in the farmhouse garden with a pipe in his mouth—no, not even when the pigs took Mr. Jones's clothes out of the wardrobes and put them on, Napoleon himself appearing in a black coat, ratcatcher breeches, and leather leggings, while his favourite sow appeared in the watered silk dress which Mrs. Jones had been used to wear on Sundays.

A week later, in the afternoon, a number of dogcarts drove up to the farm. A deputation of neighbouring farmers had been invited to make a tour of inspection. They were shown all over the farm, and expressed great admiration for everything they saw, especially the windmill. The animals were weeding the turnip field. They worked diligently, hardly raising their faces from the ground, and not knowing whether to be more frightened of the pigs or of the human visitors.

That evening loud laughter and bursts of singing came from the farmhouse. And suddenly, at the sound of the mingled voices, the animals were stricken with curiosity. What could be happening in there, now that for the first time animals and human beings were meeting on terms of equality? With one accord they began to creep as quietly as possible into the farmhouse garden.

At the gate they paused, half frightened to go on but Clover led the way in. They tiptoed up to the house, and such animals as were tall enough peered in at the dining-room window. There, round the long table, sat half a dozen farmers and half a dozen of the more eminent pigs, Napoleon himself occupying the seat of honour at the head of the table. The pigs appeared completely at ease in their chairs The company had been enjoying a game of cards but had broken off for the moment, evidently in order to drink a toast. A large jug was circulating, and the mugs were being refilled with beer. No one noticed the wondering faces of the animals that gazed in at the window.

Mr. Pilkington, of Foxwood, had stood up, his mug in his hand. In a moment, he said, he would ask the present company to drink a toast. But before doing so, there were a few words that he felt it incumbent upon him to say.

It was a source of great satisfaction to him, he said—and, he was sure, to all others present—to feel that a long period of mistrust and misunderstanding had now come to an end. There had been a time—not that he, or any of the present company, had shared such sentiments—but there had been a time when the respected proprietors of Animal Farm had been regarded, he would not say with hostility, but perhaps with a certain measure of misgiving, by their human neighbours. Unfortunate incidents had occurred, mistaken ideas had been current. It had been felt that the existence of a farm owned and operated by pigs was somehow abnormal and was liable to have an unsettling effect in the neighbourhood. Too many farmers had assumed, without due enquiry, that on such a farm a spirit of licence and indiscipline would prevail. They had been nervous about the effects upon their own animals, or even upon their human employees. But all such doubts were now dispelled. Today he and his friends had visited Animal Farm and inspected every inch of it with their own eyes, and what did they find? Not only the most up-to-date methods, but a discipline and an orderliness which should be an example to all farmers everywhere. He believed that he was right in saying that the lower animals on Animal Farm did more work and received less food than any animals in the county. Indeed, he and his fellow-visitors today had observed many features which they intended to introduce on their own farms immediately.

He would end his remarks, he said, by emphasising once again the friendly feelings that subsisted, and ought to subsist, between Animal Farm and its neighbours. Between pigs and human beings there was not, and there need not be, any clash of interests whatever. Their struggles and their difficulties were one. Was not the labour problem the same everywhere? Here it became apparent that Mr. Pilkington was about to spring some carefully prepared witticism on the company, but for a moment he was too overcome by amusement to be able to utter it. After much choking, during which his various chins turned purple, he managed to get it out: "If you have your lower animals to contend with," he said, "we have our lower classes!" *This bon mot* set the table in a roar;

and Mr. Pilkington once again congratulated the pigs on the low rations, the long working hours, and the general absence of pampering which he had observed on Animal Farm.

And now, he said finally, he would ask the company to rise to their feet and make certain that their glasses were full. "Gentlemen," concluded Mr. Pilkington, "gentlemen, I give you a toast: To the prosperity of Animal Farm!"

There was enthusiastic cheering and stamping of feet. Napoleon was so gratified that he left his place and came round the table to clink his mug against Mr. Pilkington's before emptying it. When the cheering had died down, Napoleon, who had remained on his feet, intimated that he too had a few words to say.

Like all of Napoleon's speeches, it was short and to the point. He too, he said, was happy that the period of misunderstanding was at an end. For a long time there had been rumours—circulated, he had reason to think, by some malignant enemy—that there was something subversive and even revolutionary in the outlook of himself and his colleagues. They had been credited with attempting to stir up rebellion among the animals on neighbouring farms. Nothing could be further from the truth! Their sole wish, now and in the past, was to live at peace and in normal business relations with their neighbours. This farm which he had the honour to control, he added, was a co-operative enterprise. The title-deeds, which were in his own possession, were owned by the pigs jointly.

He did not believe, he said, that any of the old suspicions still lingered, but certain changes had been made recently in the routine of the farm which should have the effect of promoting confidence stiff further. Hitherto the animals on the farm had had a rather foolish custom of addressing one another as "Comrade." This was to be suppressed. There had also been a very strange custom, whose origin was unknown, of marching every Sunday morning past a boar's skull which was nailed to a post in the garden. This, too, would be suppressed, and the skull had already been buried. His visitors might have observed, too, the green flag which flew from the masthead. If so, they would perhaps have noted that the white hoof and horn with which it had previously been marked had now been removed. It would be a plain green flag from now onwards.

He had only one criticism, he said, to make of Mr. Pilkington's excellent and neighbourly speech. Mr. Pilkington had referred throughout to "Animal Farm." He could not of course know—for he, Napoleon, was only now for the first time announcing it—that the name "Animal Farm" had been abolished. Henceforward the farm was to be known as "The Manor Farm"—which, he believed, was its correct and original name.

"Gentlemen," concluded Napoleon, "I will give you the same toast as before, but in a different form. Fill your glasses to the brim. Gentlemen, here is my toast: To the prosperity of The Manor Farm! "

There was the same hearty cheering as before, and the mugs were emptied to the dregs. But as the animals outside gazed at the scene, it seemed to them that some strange thing was happening. What was it that had altered in the faces of the pigs? Clover's old dim eyes flitted from one face to another. Some of them had five chins, some had four, some had three. But what was it that seemed to be melting and changing? Then, the applause having come to an end, the company took up their cards and continued the game that had been interrupted, and the animals crept silently away.

But they had not gone twenty yards when they stopped short. An uproar of voices was coming from the farmhouse. They rushed back and looked through the window again. Yes, a violent quarrel was in progress. There were shoutings, bangings on the table, sharp suspicious glances, furious denials. The source of the trouble appeared to be that Napoleon and Mr. Pilkington had each played an ace of spades simultaneously.

Twelve voices were shouting in anger, and they were all alike. No question, now, what had happened to the faces of the pigs. The creatures outside looked from pig to man, and from man to pig, and from pig to man again; but already it was impossible to say which was which.